Daught
of the
Mountain

Un Cuento
by Edna Escamill

aunt lute books

SAN FRANCISCO

First Edition 10-9-8-7-6-5-4-3-2

Aunt Lute Books
P.O. Box 410687
San Francisco, CA 94141

Cover and text design: Pam Wilson Design Studio
Map and cover artwork: Debra DeBondt
Cover photograph: Rio Grande Blanket, 1880-1900 L.5.62.79—
Collection of the Spanish Colonial Arts Society, Inc.; courtesy of
the Museum of New Mexico Press and the Museum of Interna-
tional Folk Art, from their book *Spanish Textile Tradition of New
Mexico and Colorado.*
Editor: Joan Pinkvoss
Production: Eileen Anderson
      Jayna Brown
      Robin Candace
      Martha Davis
      Nancy Fishman
      Gina Kaufer
      Kathleen Wilkinson
Typesetting: Debra DeBondt

Printed in the U.S.A. on acid-free paper

This book is an Aunt Lute Foundation educational project and
was supported by a grant from the National Endowment for the
Arts. The Aunt Lute Foundation is the non-profit entity that grew
out of Spinsters/Aunt Lute Book Company.

This is a work of fiction. In no way does it intend to represent
any real person, living or dead, or any real incidents.

Library of Congress Cataloging-in-Publication Data

Escamill, Edna, 1942-
   Daughter of the mountain : un cuento / by Edna
Escamill.—1st ed.
     p.   cm.
    ISBN 1-879960-07-9 (trade paper : acid-free) : $8.95.—
   ISBN 1-879960-08-7 (lib. bdg. : acid-free) : $18.95
    1. Yaqui Indians—Fiction.   I. Title.
PS3555.S26D38   1991
813'.54—dc20
                 91-9754
                 CIP

Acknowledgements

▲

My sincere thanks

To those many women who over the years have helped me make my way;

To the few who read this story in its ragged beginnings and gave me courage to continue; especially Joan Pinkvoss, my editor, who acted like "sure, why not?" and made me believe it too;

To all those women at Aunt Lute Books who labored on the production of this book with intensity of purpose and with heart—*con el mismo corazón les doi las gracias*, with the same heart I give thanks to all of you;

To both my grandmothers, one of native blood and one of european, who fed my understanding of both worlds;

To my dear son, Eden, for sharing my life and listening to my stories;

And to the Arizona/Sonora desert and her mountains, my teacher and my refuge, the source of my life and of this story.

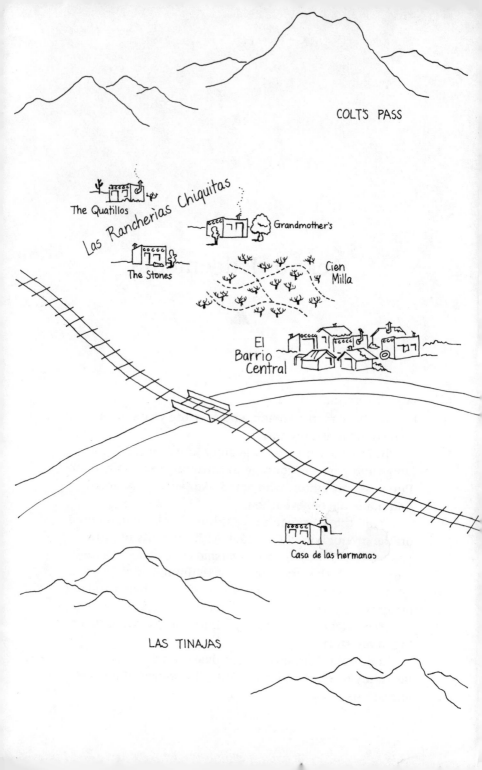

COLT'S PASS

The Quatillos

Las Rancherias Chiquitas

Grandmother's

The Stones

Cien Milla

El Barrio Central

Casa de las hermanas

LAS TINAJAS

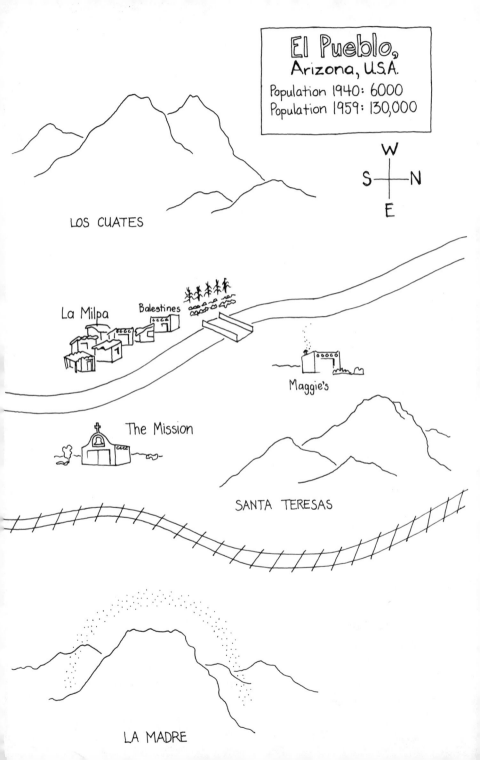

A note about the Spanish in this novel: where the Spanish appears in *italics*, it indicates the beginning of a conversation that *takes place entirely in Spanish;* where Spanish is interspersed with English in everyday conversation, it is not italicized.

Invocation

▲

Blessed Mother,
ancient and eternal goddess,
guardian of the earth,
Be with us.

El Amanecer

Hija de mi sangre y de mi corazón, ahora te voy a contar algo. Pero las palabras de este cuento, como yo, no vienen de tu mundo. Son almas de recuerdos, escondidas en un aparecer de espíritus. Son brisas en ojos que lloran. Al acordarnos tenemos esperanzas y jugamos a las escondidas una con la otra. Entonces esta historia la retengo en el mundo solamente para tus oídos y para tus ojos: Bueno, ese día no fue como todos. Fue el día en que me habló La Madre de mi verdadero nombre. Nunca me había hablado en voz y la tuve que obedecer. Ella quiso que andara en el mundo nuevo donde viven puras palabras y donde yo estaba muda. Ese día al oir mi nombre me arrastré al lugar donde hay una ventana en la sierra. Al alcanzar las lomas comencé a escupir el daño de mi ser. Y comencé a vivir. Comencé a hablar.

At Daybreak

Daughter of my blood and of my heart, I'm going to tell you something. But the words of this story do not come from this world. They are the souls of memories hidden in an apparition of spirits. They are a breeze to crying eyes. In remembering we have hope and can play hide and seek with one another. Therefore I hold this story in the world only for your ears and your eyes: So, that day was not like any other. It was the day La Madre called me by my real name. She had never spoken to me in that way and I had to obey her. She determined that I walk in this new world where words live and where I was dumb. That day when I heard my name I dragged myself to the place where there is a window in the mountain. When I reached the hills I began to vomit the damage from my being. I began to live. I began to speak.

Chapter 1

▲

A long time ago before you were born El Pueblo was small and people lived in scattered rancherías surrounded by desert and mountains.

One morning in those days the smell of water which is on its way is in the desert air but it is barely dawn, too soon to be concerned about a storm coming. A touch of woodsmoke lingers between the sloping plain and small peaks to the southeast. Just to the south of El Pueblo hidden from view by a natural bajada is a ramada. A small adobe house rests in its shadow. Beyond the ramada is a bare flat place and there smoke is rising from a comal where a mesquite fire is burning. While she waits for the comal to be ready, the tortilla maker Consuelo, a strong woman in her middle years, stands with legs far apart and her large arms in the folds of her apron. She is watching the glow of the rising sun chase the darkness from the peaks.

She bends to check the coals, carefully testing the surface of her comal and, judging it ready, she removes her rebozo and lays it folded on a table. She brings the bandeja covered with white cloth and puts it on the chair next to the comal. She takes a ball of dough and kneads it between her fingers until it is a small circle and begins to pat it between her hands back and forth, one to the other. When the tortilla is larger than her hands she swings it forearm to forearm, all the while stretching it with her fingers, then swings it onto the comal. The tortilla bubbles instantly. She lifts one corner with calloused fingers, shifts it around to cook evenly and flips it over. She presses out the steam with a clean white cloth. When the tortilla is cooked she wraps it in a cloth alongside the masa in the bandeja. She works quickly, stopping only once to stir the nuggets of coals and make flames flash out. The morning sun is now coming and she lowers her tapalo a little more over her eyes and slaps the last ball of dough between her palms. The crisp motion of her wrist, the smell of burning flour, the shifting transparent quality of the air above the comal and the hard brown surface of the earth around her—these things move around and through her being. Her eyes contain distances. Standing there in her grey shirt with tiny white flowers and a long black skirt, she looks like weathered wood.

Her labor finished, she pauses. She listens to the faraway sound of the wind. She hears the trilling of the desert mockingbird, El Shonte celebrating the morning. He sings out loudly to the desert and tears energetically at the paper beneath his feet. Watching him deny his captivity when there is no cage, Consuelo is gripped by a vision that shows the shape of another existence enclosing him, taking away his wildness. She suddenly hears hoofbeats and she is seized by a shudder in her chest. As though someone walks on her grave. She crosses herself and at the same moment hears her sister's voice from the house—what is Consuelo doing standing there like a sonsa? As if there is nothing to do? The tortilla maker gathers her things hurriedly and walks quickly to the house.

"*Cómo le gusta a ésta perder el tiempo.* How this one likes to waste time," mutters Emma. Her own small body is always in motion. She has already uncovered her canaries, fed and watered them, whispering "Muchachitos" and "Bonitos." Her sewing machine has been going for an hour and she has finished preparing el desayuno because Josepha is going into town on business today.

Meanwhile Consuelo hesitates at the door to gaze once more in the direction of the hediondilla. Each bush, each cholla with its glowing thorns seems to grow, coming close. Balancing the bandeja on one hip, Consuelo shades her eyes trying to see better, experiencing the sensation of stepping forward into the palo verde surrounding the ramada. It is as though El Camino de los Dioses was approaching. She is frightened by her own thoughts and crosses herself again.

Josepha and Emma are already seated at the table waiting impatiently for the tortillas. Always tight with every speck of food, Emma tears a tortilla into quarters and places one piece emphatically near each plate. Josepha is cracking her soft-boiled egg with the edge of her spoon. The oldest sister, she is the only one who has an egg because she is going into town this morning and needs her strength. Consuelo eats slowly, chewing last night's beans and quelites and enjoying the flavor of freshly made coffee. "*Debes de hacer el café nuevo cada día.* You should make the coffee fresh every day," she says to Emma.

"Sure, and what do you know?" snaps Emma. "I suppose I'm to throw away perfectly good grounds. We would soon be starving if we did things your way!"

Josepha does not comment. She finishes her egg, wipes the plate with a last fragment of tortilla and drinks the last swallow of coffee. She has already powdered her face before breakfast. Her bony chest is visible beneath the gold medallion she wears. She goes to change her cotton dress for her good black one. She is a woman of few words. With her new handkerchief in her hand and her purse pinned safely to the inside of her pocket, she takes her umbrella and is out the door. Emma calls after her to be careful and watches from the doorway until the wandering trail takes her from sight. Now these are Emma's moments: quickly clearing the table under Consuelo, she collects the tortilla scraps and a small piece of orange she has been saving and says to Consuelo, "When you finish with the dishes it would be good if you'd start with the washing before the storm comes and spoils the clothes." Then she escapes with her dish of scraps and her heart beating with anticipation. She goes to the hillside to check her shonte trap.

Climbing the hill, Emma prods the path ahead cautiously with a stick. She is watching for snakes that may be sleeping in the warm rays of the morning sun. Behind some large rocks is the trap she created for the bird she would like to have above all. The wooden crate is balanced upon a slim stick, empty. Big red ants are speeding away portions of celery tops offered as bait. Fortunately Emma's anticipation is tempered by patience of purpose. She sweeps the ground between two young saguaros with a palo verde branch and sets out the fresh bait. El Shonte will not succeed in reaching the orange he loves with his long beak; he will have to go in the box and trip the string. She looks hopefully around at the tallest cactus, listening for the familiar whistle of the mockingbird. A chilling breeze still blows from places deep in shadow and Emma tightens her rebozo around her shoulders. I must return to my sewing, she thinks. There is much to do this day. Pero la verdad es that she is not comfortable this far from the shelter of the house. The mountains are too great, too strong; she is dizzy looking up at the sky. She descends the hill almost running clasping her rebozo to her breast, anxious to be indoors again with her birds and her sewing.

In El Pueblo things are just beginning to wake up. The vaqueros who came to town the night before are feeling their way outside to clear their throats and spit in the street. Then they will lean against the blue tiles of the new Bus Station that faces east and warm their bones in the bright morning sun. From this vantage point they will be able to see all the way north and also south. They will be able to catch sight of the young señoritas coming and going with their mamas from the Mission. They will also be able to keep an eye out for any Indios trying to sneak out of town over the bridge and to kick their asses. They have each other and the best corner in El Pueblo. So by the time the sun is halfway up the new blue tiles the young men and the vaqueros are ready and waiting for action.

Down the street across from the railroad station and out of sight of that end of the street, the light is beginning to seep into a certain cold alleyway. In the heart of La Yaqui asleep against the wall of the saloon, the morning light uncoils out of the night like a cascabel coming out to sun herself. The woman's hands shudder feeling the first dusty rays of light. Without opening her eyes she sees the western hills emerging and reaching for the sun's blood. She rolls away from the wall and raises a bruised face. Pain and humiliation burning, she blindly searches for a bottle to kill the noise. With that motion she has to urinate and stumbles a way down the alleyway into the stains and stench of others. Relieved, she tries to unglue her eyes and come back to her spot where she feels a small measure of peace at the sight of the sun on the wall, the sunlight on the mountains. Sunspirit coming so she can leave this cold street and find a warm self in her walking. She stops to hear a mockingbird call; impossibly, the mountain is calling again and again naming a Name. She is naming a Being. There is a low roll of thunder bouncing forward from the rocks and La Yaqui presses herself to deaf walls to protect herself, but hands are pushing out of her, birthing cholla...her face is like raw stone...hoofbeats are the beating heart of the mountain cradled in speech...her arms opening....Thus meeting herself, la yaqui Adela Sewa doesn't notice la mexicana Josepha appear at the end of the block. That one having rounded the corner in full swing has her eyes on the Clock. After stopping briefly at the Mission to pray she has come this long way around just to see it again. The Clock she knows from her first days in this country. The marvel of it. Something so big and free for everyone to see. She is almost to the alleyway when she sees La India lying against the wall, her disordered greying hair ablaze in the sun. Startled, she turns hastily from the humanity of the eyes and from what might have been the answering beat of her own heart. "Indios cochinos," she mutters to herself and feels angry at the new law that says Indios can no longer be arrested for intoxication. She crosses abruptly to the other side of the street, quickening her steps against an indefinable feeling of possibility. *"Tomados andan todo el tiempo.* Drunk all the time!" she mutters against the haloed figure on the ground. She will think no more about it as she approaches the great Clock in front of the jewelry store. She stops beneath it to compare its time with the time of her own wristwatch, proudly noting they are the same and that she is on schedule. Just then she hears the laughter from the men on the corner. What they see is a thin woman all in black hiding a face that is no longer young behind her rebozo. They allow her to hurry around the block satisfied to wait for more worthy prey.

When La Yaqui is able to walk she goes west following Josepha's footsteps. She passes the stores with the shadow things in the glass. Looking in the windows she falls into her own face growing smaller and smaller. She cannot reach anything on the other side. She cannot touch or smell or get close to it. The things in the window are not meant for her. They belong to a cleanliness not of her skin. She looks down at the street and her stomach rises to her mouth and she clutches at the wall, holding on to it with all of the strength in her stiff fingers. And then she remembers the corner—she is an injured woman under the cold and hostile eyes of many men. Their catcalls and jeers fall on her together with spittle flying in a long unbroken stream as the men and boys clap and cheer for the one who has scored. She blinks her eyes, takes a step and almost falls. Her ankle hurts fiercely but she grips her way around the corner and away from the laughter. The vaquero called Lizard shoves his hands deep into his pockets while the younger boys watch and smirk. "Puta," he says and follows her retreating figure with another long gob of spit aimed at her back.

She knows where she is going. She needs to find her thoughts, and it is in the thing brought by the Españoles that she can rest for hours. Sometimes policemen come and look rudely into her face but then they leave her alone. She goes to a park outside the home of the policemen. This is an old place and belonged long ago to the first people of El Pueblo. Later the old Mexicans will sit beneath the wide branches of the cottonwoods dozing in the long hours of the afternoon. Those that come here now do not bother her—they too belong less and less. Their old places are filling up with buildings and there is no more room for them. So La Yaqui Adela Sewa comes by instinct and sits at the edge of the deep quiet pool and looks with expectation and wonder into a world of green waving fronds where creatures of flashing gold swim among the black rocks. Immobile, she gazes down unaware of anything else, in the midst of ancient paths and unpainted benches on the edge of town. For her this place and this thing of the fish and the water are in some way home. Free from her conscious mind her spirit moves like the Prince of Birds inside the desert wind. Soon she too can breathe in water and glide smoothly without any sound into her innermost and strongest will. At the end of the day she knows what she must do.

The day is ending. On distant rimrock rain comes to the earth at last. Cactus spines catch droplets of water and make glistening halos all over the mountain. The cactus casts green shadows complementing the orange glow of the setting sun. To Adela Sewa who is making her way along a certain trail going up to the Pass, this is the way it is: she is walking inside the belly of the world. The green light is its heart. The orange light its blood. She is walking inside a multitude of unborn worlds. Each one is the image and soul of the other. Her life is together with all the lives of the mountain. Tomorrow she will look down from a hole in the rock and see her skin stretched out flat to the edge of the world where all trails begin, where all peoples are born. This vision will be her reward. Today she is holding on for life to the knowledge that all the beings of the mountain know peace.

The light from the sun setting behind her spreads slowly up the mountain, illuminating Adela Sewa as she labors up towards a last stand of mesquite. She is suffering. Whiskey water and white death are squeezing out of her. Her guts are being wrung dry and her hands are scraped by sharp rock. And this is as it should be. It no longer matters that she is unseen in the world she has left. She pulls off her clothes and ties them in a bundle on her back. She has nothing on but the huaraches on her feet. She removes her sandals and rinses them with light powdery dirt dug from the side of the trail. The same dirt she rubs into her head, face, neck and arms down to the soles of her feet. The sun is gone now except for a streak of vermillion stretching from one end of the horizon to the other and now the sadness comes out of the darkness and wrenches her by the throat. For so long this sadness has had its way with her, consuming and twisting her into inhuman shapes, and these have stolen her face. Now, out of the darkest part of the sky, these evils are sucked to her meager life. They do not have Names of their own and they follow her up the mountain begging, pleading, condemning and cursing. They tear their hair and display ravaged bodies which she has made, pursuing her with vengeance and with unrelenting fervor. She has stumbled and fallen more times than she knows and each time these thieves who haggle over remnants of her soul chatter horribly among themselves, mimicking her pain and responding to her fear with shining carnivorous teeth. But they do not want to catch her. They only want to accompany her making a fiesta. She turns and runs at them grinning, stretching out her arms, laughing. No precious jewels, no gifts from Father Peyote, this gagging choking emptiness. She stumbles from rock to rock in the dark and feeling a warm boulder, she climbs up and lays her naked body upon it. But she cannot rest. She bloodies her fist on the rock not to feel warmth, not to feel. She wants to be dead. She has called for death many times and at last La Muerte comes and crouches beside her. She knows Death as a dense dark thing and her body recoils in terror. Her soul invites Death to come closer but her body is speechless, tearing at the rock it is forced to grip. The body would fall apart to get away but her alma, with its single pure thread of eternal life, remains firm. Her soul opens, inviting La Muerte to enter and Death enters as smoothly as flowered silk. And Death sits and feeds. She eats the shades of this Being though they beg and make promises, anything to keep their existence, but in the end La Muerte eats them down to the last lie.

Below the mountain in la ranchería de Las Hermanas night falls quickly. Consuelo is in the small space curtained off as her room. In the light from the lamp she is undoing her hair. She combs it out with the same comb that holds her hair in place. She takes the bits of her hair that remain in the comb and rolls them into a circle with her fingers. When she has grown old and loses her hair, she will make a hairpiece from the hair she has saved. She makes two braids for sleeping and then sits in silent reflection. These are the only moments when all her work is done. Through the small window she hears the chickens in their coop. Their soft murmuring sounds as they make their nest come out of the night and comfort her. She puts aside the strange vision of El Shonte in a cage. The hoofbeats coming closer are stolen by a familiar voice of thunder echoing around the feet of the mountain. She is not afraid of that. In the other part of the house, Josepha and Emma also perform their nightly ritual. They have finished with their hair and are praying. They are sitting up together in the bed they share holding their beads, praying to El Señor and to La Virgencita. The blessed little Virgin who understands all sorrows, whose tears for her Son wash away humanity's pain. Even in the golden light of the lamp Josepha is pale. Her breast rises and falls swiftly as she murmurs earnest prayers putting to rest the endeavors of the day. While saying her Santa Marías and Sálvames, she sees the faces of the suffering Christ and the Heavenly Mother, her arms laden with flowers, and disturbing pictures of the streets of El Pueblo: a man's gob of spit hanging in midair; the dark impassive face of una India crowned with the first light; her own face inside the giant Clock shrinking and shrinking...Josepha comes to herself with a start.

"*No muevas la cama!* Don't shake the bed!" Emma is too excited to remain irritated. Tomorrow she will capture her mockingbird. He is already there settled comfortably inside her trap, sated on tortilla and orange. She returns to her novena to San Judas, keeper of the flame. She prays fervently for the Padrecitos of the Mission and for the Little Sisters who are so good. She prays for the health of her precious birds, for their innocent souls. In giving thanks for their daily bread she cannot help a small squirm of ill feeling towards Consuelo who is so wasteful God will punish all of them.

Josepha speaks shortly, "*Ya acabastes?* Are you finished?" Emma quickly kisses her cross and puts her rosary around her neck. The lamp is out. Las Hermanas lie looking into the darkness. Emma sees a tiny glow from the direction of Consuelo's room and mumbles, "There she is wasting fuel!" Josepha grunts and turns over closing her eyes and ears on everything.

Finally the house is dark. From far away a breath of sage touches the roof and the house shakes. Their bodies sense it and know it for the blessing it is and are at peace.

That night as she sleeps far above the desert in the hole in the rock, the same sage wind touches la yaqui Adela Sewa lightly. The wind has traveled far; the day before it was in the region known as the Sea of Cortés in the wilderness of Baja pursuing sea lions playing among the harsh black rocks. La Yaqui dreams that the desert beneath her is a rolling sea. She swims and forces her frightened and exhausted body to the safety of the shallows. She awakens and is chilled by the wind. A bright slice of moon is overhead and in the valley the cry of a coyote carries to the top of the mountain. La Yaqui covers herself with sage branches. Curled up against a slab of rock she stares at the moon and remembers her first years. From long and far away her memories speak to her now in her heart. Inside their jacal she hears every shift of the wind, El Río Yaqui moaning sweetly behind cricket voices and the melodious sounds of her mother's gourds hanging from one corner of the roof. With every shift of the wind her heart becomes more alive....

El Cuento:

Tenías nueve meses cuando dijiste tu primera palabra. Muy claro dijiste "Milk, milk" en Inglés. Pero no volviste a hablar una palabra. Tenías más de tres años y no hablabas. Entonces te llevaron con doctores y no te encontraron nada. Al fin una curandera dijo que te llevara a la entrada del cañón y a la pura subida de la luna llena que te metiera una llave de esqueleto en la boca y le diera una vuelta. Pues te soltaste hablando.

The Story:

You said your first word when you were nine months old. Very clearly you said "Milk, milk" in English. But you didn't say another word. You were more than three years old and you didn't talk. Then you were taken to doctors but they didn't find anything wrong. At last a healer said to take you to the mouth of the canyon and exactly when the full moon rises, to put a skeleton key in your mouth and turn it. Well, you started talking right away.

Chapter 2

The little girl heard the sound the wind made among desert things all the time. Each tough green thing rising up out of the spare desert earth. Whole pieces of sharp rock biting upwards. Bold faces of mountains thrust at the sky's blue awareness. She listened to the immensity and heard the music of dry branches rasping across the rocky floors of long tight canyons. Heard the freedom of tumbleweeds flying bouncing racing each other inside the wind.

Things moved against other things: she knew the world inside by the world outside giving birth too; stretching blood, air, tissue, water. Knew the gentle internal force of the rain from out of the wind. From out of the dust and storm. She looked down and along the row of funnel shaped little holes discovery shining.

She was squatting in the dirt just under roof cover. The rain was sweeping mightily across the pink earth everywhere. The rain was falling so much and so hard the prickly pear and the pomegranate trees were first gone and then back again. Back and forth. The rain came down noisily in torrents streaming off the roof but right there in front of her was a long row of perfect little holes the size of her finger. Where did they come from? Catching one drop of water flying from above *landing in a hole*. Drops along the porch. All of her knew that happens and then this happens. But before she knew it there were only the beautifully round and deep little holes. Many all in a row lined up. Each one had walls that went straight up made of the thinnest earth. She touched one carefully inside and out. It didn't break. Each one looked and felt almost the same. They were here. They were made and they were not for anything. They were perfectly themselves. And they were beautiful.

This information was without words. This information was all pictures: a drop in midflight, a hole appearing. Up there fat rolling clouds and across it a flash and slash, whole skythunder on the head of her roof. It was sky moving fast. Dust coming, floating in the little air left between fat round hot drops. Faster and faster more of them. Licking her face. Rain curtains out there across a big space full of stickers cactus rocks red soil naked ground. She wasn't getting too wet where she was sitting. And the rain water made white curtains waving backwards and forewards in front of her and *loud* it came straight down drumming. And it *stopped!* And the earth, the desert was still there. The water streamed away in crooked little rivers, rushing fast and rushing less—rivulets quickly passing. The clouds rolled big. They came out of the pouring rain that was gone. But now they were pink and very white and grey and round. Big rounds and little rounds following bunches of rounds having blue pieces of sky close and far in back where the sun was setting. That was how the clouds made different colors.

Before the sun went away it shone down on her from between the clouds. Golden streaming sun on the perfect little holes. It lit up the green fleshy cactus. It polished the dirt brown and stuck to the water and made sparking-mud. The sky got more and more white; where the clouds were it set. It just happened. Now. She was squatting on the ground and there was rain and not rain and shining bluegreen and brownlight happening.

And oh, the little round dirt holes were still here with her.

Chapter 3

▲

Late one afternoon word spread like fire through the jacales of La Milpa of all they were going to give over at the new warehouses. People scurried here and there excitedly telling one another about it. The women in their loose-fitting sleeveless dresses gathering together with their friends; the children milling about and running from one bunch to another talking about it, what there will be, where it is, exciting each other to go. So, after a supper that was somewhat hurried for most of them, small groups of people, mostly women and children, set out from La Milpa to the new warehouses in El Pueblo.

"They're going to give free samples of everything the trucks will be carrying, 'mano," said one boy to another. Bale promised his little brother he'd get some for him too, and Eddie gave him a wobbly hug back. The people brought paper sacks to put everything in and they walked across the bridge and wove their way through the first small streets of El Pueblo. Most of them knew how to go because they had been to fiestas at the Armory Park. So they cut across vacant lots and up alleyways and walked gingerly in the streets going by the houses where the rich viejitos lived, the ones who came from the East to cure their diseases in the Arizona sun. They walked along the streets not wanting to pass too near the rich two-story houses with their cement sidewalks and water sprinklers going incessantly, watering the cropped lawns and the cement sidewalks. But Bale led the kids in twisting away from their mamas' hands to run squealing under the sprinklers and then run after their mamas who walked even faster with many a sideways and backward glance at the shuttered windows and the white curtains of the viejitos who must have been asleep because no one saw them.

Cool smells came from those houses, strange smells of electric coolers and moist air and medicinal swabbed floors like nothing the children were familiar with, except in the nurse's office at school. But finally they passed the houses and crossed through the park and the yard of the old school and came to the place where the semitrucks unloaded their cargos. Even though it wasn't night yet, big yellow lights were blazing up and down the row of new warehouses and they were getting ready to turn on a spotlight. All the kids, Maggie too, gathered around the spotlight, jumping over the big thick cords running from inside the building. It looked like a giant lightbulb and when it came on there was a tremendous ooohhh and back-stepping away by the children, mesmerized by the shaft of white light leaving the glass and disappearing into the sky. Then one of the older boys yelled, *"Allí está!* There it is!" pointing, and they saw the spotlight arching across the darkening sky. People were getting in lines holding their paper bags open and the workmen were putting cajitas in each one, little white boxes filled with things they had never eaten before, things the Americanos ate only at breakfast time, little pieces of puffed things with sugar on them and different kinds of flakes. The people went from one line to another, the women pulling up their skirts and climbing up on the high platforms where the cardboard boxes were unloaded from the trucks, and the men from La Milpa who had been given this work, one or two, gave the women extra cajitas and looked the other way when they saw the same faces more than once in the same line.

All evening more groups of people came across the desert towards the row of new warehouses and loaded up on cereal boxes and bright new pencils with writing on them they didn't understand. The spotlight rode back and forth across the broad desert sky making it impossible to see the stars. And finally, when they had eaten as many cajitas of stuff as they could stand and packed away as many little boxes as their bags could hold, and the children had as many pencils as they could stick in their Levi's, the crowds began to diminish and the women and children from La Milpa began straggling back across las calles towards the west. The boys and girls walked with their necks twisted around and tried walking backwards so they could keep watching the spotlight going from one end of the sky to the other.

Everyone was in good spirits because they had been given free things and the gringos in charge with their white faces like ghosts in the glare of bright lights, with their short colorless hair shouting instructions to each other across the space of warehouses, had seemed to be waiting for them. And had even looked directly at them as the cajitas went into their sacks, acknowledging and welcoming these Mexicans from across the Río, not seeming to mind that they were speaking Spanish a mile a minute and had descended on them like cucarachas on a hunk of panocha. The people had enjoyed themselves and they were not afraid of the night walking back along the unfamiliar streets, walking quickly by the houses of the viejitos on the sidewalk this time.

Maggie saw that the houses where the rich viejitos lived had lights on in all the windows. And in all the porches lights burned. She had never seen so many lights on, not lámparas but real lightbulbs burning, and some of the houses had their doors open so the people could be seen sitting on their sofas listening to the radio, or reading newspapers on big sillones, or sitting at their tables with other individuals eating or playing cards.

Maggie could not believe they had their lights on and their doors open and were not concerned with who might be looking in. They were not afraid of wasting electricidad. They did not worry about leaving the light on in rooms they were not in! They did not carry the light with them carefully from room to room.

Maggie hung back wanting to see an old couple sitting across from each other at their dining table. She inched toward them across the wet grass and was crouching there, afraid to get closer, when Bale whispered, "Ca'mere," and they went on all fours up the steps one by one until their noses were almost pressed against the screen. "They can't see us," said Bale. Then he said, "Let's get out of here," and started backing down the stairs. "I want to see," said Maggie, standing her ground. She was ashamed of the way everyone hurried by these strange houses in the dark. She wanted to be like the people inside, wanted to keep lights burning in all the rooms just because she wanted to. Wanted to feel so sure about everything that the front door could always stay open to the darkness. She wondered what it would be like to be like that. She wondered what such people were like, to have things to say across a richly polished table. And then moving stealthily away she felt all the more her difference. The difference of her people from these sitting in their well-lighted rooms. Because of the things, the fat furniture, the white walls, the coolers and the curtains, the dishes filled with unknown foods, the cards, the rugs, the shining floors and the way the people were—the calm way they exposed themselves without fear, without a thought—*because of the way they left their doors open and their lights on*, she felt like she didn't know who these others, her people, the mexicanos, were and why they were different. They were poor and they suffered from the heat, the cold, from hunger and from each other. She didn't know why. She didn't know why she was ashamed. She was ashamed at wanting to be like the rich viejitos were who had eyeglasses to see what they couldn't see. She was ashamed at hanging there in the dark without them knowing or maybe not liking it.

So she ran away from the open door and the sidewalks and the wet green grass and ran until she caught up to the voices she knew. She ran across the bridge to the barking of the dogs, happy to see the small dark and squat jacales with their tipsy stove pipes, the tiny clouded windows high up and the flickering light of oil lamps burning spots of gold in the darkness. Happy to be with Grandmother, to see she still looked the same. Her rebozo over her head and around her shoulders, her grey blouse with the sleeves ending above the large wrists, her long black skirt and the look and feel of the brown hand holding her own securely. Maggie opened to the smells of the night, the honeysuckle smell along the riverbed. The stars zoomed in the far black as they walked along the edge of El Barrio Central towards las rancherías, savoring the night, the smell and depth of it as if the darkness were alive and breathing.

It was the desert around them. Here where no lights burned except occasionally and far in the distance. Here where there was nothing electric, where no radios filled the space. Where there were few houses and the few grew sparser still. They walked on a trail surrounded by mesquite and sage. She felt the small colored rocks under her feet, the solid desert that also moved and yielded to her. She smelled the stems and leaves of resinous sage bushes and she breathed the air in places filled with the powdery sauco Grandmother used to make tea for her kidneys.

The feathery needles of the palo verde waved in the breezes and she heard the tiny rustlings of small nocturnal animals nosing about, the little pack rats with their cheeks bulging with seeds unafraid of humans as they passed by without noise. And the jackrabbit standing on his hind legs at attention and then dashing away into the bushes. She felt them going deeper into the darkness resonant with cricket song following the silver night moths who danced like wisps of moonlight searching for the blossoms that held life.

The earth in all directions was Maggie's safety. She could not touch the stars but they sparkled to her yearning.

They stopped in the darkest part of the desert as they had many times before. They stopped to feel the life around them and to gaze at the mystery of stars strewn in cosmic play through countless years and dimensions. Wordless happiness enveloped Maggie, a headiness of delight until she thought she would topple over and find herself not on the ground but in the sky among fiery living souls. So there in the middle of the trail she sat down in the dirt grabbing her ankles and laughing. Grandmother said nothing peering into the desert sniffing what came from the mountains. The wind quality changed as it flew and fluttered from palo verde to mesquite, swooping and questing among intentional designs made by countless thorns on the countless bodies, tall and squat, bent or curving or straight, of ribbed, thick-skinned cacti. Suddenly Maggie jumped up and down, wanting to catapult from the earth into the bits of fire. The small fists she held outstretched to the world unclenched. For these moments her hands opened. She did not resist. She wanted to sink down into the body of the desert too and gather all the beanpods she knew, crooked tree limbs and naked earth and press them into her chest. She wanted to eat up the desert and that is what she was doing, eating of the soullife around her. It made her want to burst apart with joy. Until Grandmother put a quieting hand on her head, saying, "*Quieta, quieta*. Be calm. I don't want you to get lost." They stood together for a little while longer and then Grandmother took her hand once more and they continued along the trail to the ranchería.

That night after Maggie was asleep, Grandmother dumped the bag and the remaining cajitas, filled with something puffed with sugar on it, into the fire.

Chapter 4

▲

Suddenly they heard the wind gust against the house. *"Hay viene la tormenta!* The storm is coming!" said Grandmother. Maggie ran to the door ahead of her. From there she saw the mountains and a great cloud of dust racing towards them across the desert. Giant tumbleweeds uprooted by the strength of the wind were skimming back and forth inside the dust. They just had time to secure the doors, pushing against the force of the wind. The old woman and the child grabbed rags and old clothes and stuffed them under the doors and along the edges of the windows. The winds shook the house and rattled the windows, filling the air with fine choking dust. They waited for the rain to come, trying to breathe as little as possible. The sound of individual raindrops increased to the racket of a downpour. Then the dust settled and began to clear. Moving aside the curtain, Maggie looked out at waves of rain; the storm was directly over their heads now as bolt after bolt of lightning fell into the earth around the house. The thunder was so loud it seemed like the house was going to shake apart. At last the thunder began to sound from farther and farther away. The rain diminished. Maggie ran excitedly to the door. "No! Not yet!" shouted Grandmother. She held Maggie back and listened at the door. Then she let the child pull the door open. A fine spray of rain hit Maggie in the face. She looked up at the great boiling clouds. A few more big drops splashed down from the rolling clouds as they passed overhead. The smell of sage and the sound of rushing water filled Maggie and she ran toward the wash to the east shouting, "I'm going to get wet!" She sank up to her knees in sandy swirling water. Her long legs stood against the current. She surveyed the red earth. Along the banks the deep marks of hoofprints filled with water, flattening out in the wake of the storm. A bright green palo verde was waving in the wind. The whole world was cooled. Everything under the wind and the rain—people, tumbleweed and earth, the weathered ironwood and the mountains and sharp quartz beneath them and the saguaro standing immobile under the sky.

Maggie jumped against the gusts of wind and rain, splashing the water, feeling it wrap itself around her body. Grandmother's grey eyes watched from the house. She saw the dancing white cloud like a Great White Horse rearing up again and again, fading away in the tail of the storm. And Maggie played in the late afternoon sun that shone like a new day coloring everything. The clouds moved west and lay stretched in purple layers along the foothills. This was Maggie's world and she lived inside of it touching its life with her life. There was no room for anything else.

El Cuento:

Venía un probrecito de Margdalena y tenía unas mulas con pacas. Paró a un lado de El Pueblo e hizo campo. Unos ladrones dijeron, a la mejor éste tiene oro en las pacas. Entonces vinieron a robarle y lo mataron para quitarle el oro pero no tenía nada. Lo único que tenía en las pacas era maíz, granos de maíz. Pues lo dejaron muerto tirado allí en el camino. Entonces unas mujeres de El Pueblo vinieron y lo enterraron donde cayó. Y despues venían y le rezaban y empezó a hacer milagros. Entonces le llamaron El Tidadito a este lugar, por el que quedó tirado.

The Story:

A poor man was coming along from Margdalena and he had some mules with packs. He stopped at the edge of El Pueblo to make camp. Some thieves said to each other, I bet he has gold in those packs. So they came in the night to steal and they killed him to get the gold but there wasn't any. The only thing he had in the packs was corn, grains of corn. Well, they left him lying there dead. Then some women came from El Pueblo and buried him there where he had fallen. After that they would come and pray to him there and he began to make miracles. Then this place was called El Tidadito, the place where one was left.

Chapter 5

▲

Maggie followed Grandmother through the desert. Looking back she could still see the whitewashed walls of Las
Rancherías Chiquitas rising above the desert. Smoke
drifted aimlessly up into the cold air. Grandmother held
her rebozo tightly around her nose and mouth, her strong
shoulders bending forward against the wind whipping
around them blowing the dust in their faces. A sudden
remolino, a whirlwind materialized nearby, sending its
funnel high swirling with dust and brush. Grandmother
shouted at Maggie to follow her and cut in another
direction. She would go far out of her way to avoid being
caught in a remolino, believing them to be evil walking on
earth. The remolino zigzagged away from them, dying
down and reappearing elsewhere in another part of the
desert.

"*Abuelita, van con nosotros Las Hermanas?* Grandmother, are Las Hermanas going with us?"

"No."

"Why not?"

"Because they don't believe in him."

"Why?"

"Because his soul is outside the Church."

In spite of the wind, the sun got warmer. And then the
wind stopped and there was only the sun. Maggie's arm
felt like it was burning. The ground was hot. The rocks
sparkled. They followed the trail with their heads down,
looking where their feet were going or straight ahead but
never up at the sun. The ground abruptly sloped up onto
hard packed ground. Maggie liked the ground going up
and down. It was an empty place with no trees or mesquites or even cactus. Just hard ground. They were here
to light a candle for El Tidadito. It was at the edge of the
Barrio they were going, in the oldest part of El Pueblo
where the adobe houses were falling down but some
people still lived there. El Tidadito was on a corner where
there were no people. There were two walls making an L
shape. One wall belonged to a house and the other was
the rear of another long since gone to rubble. Into the
holes in the walls where adobes had fallen out, people put
candles. Candles on top of candles. The adobes were
covered with yellow wax, puddles hardened into streams.
Many veladoras were burning all over. Some candles were
only a bit of wax with the wick still burning. The veladoras
were white and bumpy or red, blue, yellow; tall ones with
pictures of La Guadalupe or El Santo Niño on them or
Jesus's bleeding heart.

A dog jumped at them suddenly from behind the wall,
growling at them ferociously, his black fur bristling in
anger. Maggie, terrified, grabbed at Grandmother's skirts,
twisting her around in her fear as the dog came at them

showing his fangs. Instead of backing away, Grandmother advanced towards him shouting and swinging her stick. The dog ran away looking back and barking.

"Don't be afraid of dogs," Grandmother told Maggie, who was already climbing over the adobes and playing with the warm candle wax. Grandmother made her stop and get the broom to sweep the ground. Maggie easily swept away the dust and twigs. Grandmother set her candle into the wall and they knelt down on the hard ground. Grandmother explained that this was a holy place because El Tidadito was innocent and so many believed in him. This was for prayers you wouldn't go to church for, she says. This was for prayers church couldn't answer; for something special that needed to be answered. Grandmother got up, wrapped her rebozo around her and walked away. Maggie scrambled off her knees and still looking back at the candles burning ran to catch up to her. They had come all this way just to light a candle, to kneel down and then to walk all the way back to la ranchería and Grandmother did not even look back.

Maggie wanted there to be more. She wanted to talk to somebody. Now the wind was blowing again in their faces and they would have to walk without stopping. They would have to go all the way back in one gulp. But Grandmother did not even look back to see if she was coming. The little girl with her braids flying in the wind ran behind her, stumbling on rocks and kicking them aside without looking up.

Chapter 6

▲

It was early morning, just past dawn in El Pueblo. The people were standing in a long double line in front of the Mission, waiting for Padre Pedro and the altar boys. More people came out of the church and got in line. Mostly women in black wearing rebozos or tapalos on their heads and girls with their mothers' second best scarf tied on their heads. Worn out women, men with lined faces speaking in undertones, children staring and silent. And then the priest came out carrying a huge heavy gold cross and after him, the altar boys. Maggie was astounded to see that one of them was Bale carrying a wooden cross, and another boy from El Barrio Central was carrying the incense. She squeezed in behind them but Bale didn't turn around. She saw him clenching his teeth. Mrs. Balestine in front looked severely at Maggie and made a sign at Bale just in case he was thinking of saying anything.

The sky was bright and the cassocks of the priest and the altar boys were glaring white as they led the procession west over the bridge. There were small puddles of water in El Río. Tall green weeds that had taken advantage of the sparse autumn rains grew in profusion along the riverbanks. The Padre carried the gold cross high for all those following to see. There was no talking or laughing. Eyes were held down and lips moved only in prayer. Maggie tried to keep sight of Bale but too many people got in the way and Josepha was frowning at her to be serious. Emma, her nina, smiled at her and gave her a rosary to hold. Her mama did not pay attention to her but was murmuring prayers. The Padre's sandals slapped the dust. The sun had already eaten what was left of the dawn chill as they reached the foothills of Los Quates and turned south along the dirt road leading to the grotto in the desert.

El Día de los Muertos. The day belonged to the dead. The prayers were for them. Maggie did not pray. She looked at the women and the dark men in their best heavy dark pants. She knew the ones from La Milpa, and the Quatillos were there and Mr. and Mrs. Carrillo from the rancherías, praying for their boy in Korea. Some of the women had bellies sticking out, fat with child. The old women, the grandmothers, shuffled along at the end of the line with the youngest boys of the family. The bratty boys toed the line for their abuelitas, keeping their eyes on the hem of the skirts which reached down to ankles and to tops of black shoes. Though it was not for anyone to see, the old women had worn their best stockings. Their clothes were well pressed. The night before they had heated the irons on the wood stove. Then they had attached a wooden handle to one iron at a time, using it until the heat ran out, putting it back on the stove and using another. In this way Mariana had ironed Maggie's clothes for the next day too, for this important day.

The way to the grotto in the desert was long. It took hours of walking. But it was an honor for the living and a gift to the dead. The time was spent saying prayers for the descanso, the rest of the dead, and building up indulgences for the living. It was a day for remembering. A day to recognize the dead among them. They would see this in the face of La Virgen holding El Cristo. Her face would be the face of the Queen of Heaven. Her face was that of a Queen who was also a mother. It was her mother's face they were meant to see on the day her Son was taken down from the cross. Her mother's heart burned with the fire of love for Him but His heart had stopped burning. His heart was dead. The fire would not be burning in His chest. This was what the people were going to remember way up there on the hill beyond the cemetery. To see all this they must first pass through the desert and the sun was getting hotter. Some of the men lifted up their youngest children, but most of them walked. Finally the children ventured to say once, "Tengo hambre," or "Water, Mama." At first they were ignored. The little ones were dragged along or left to make a slower way behind. But no one cried or whined. Mariana held Maggie's hand tightly. She concentrated on taking care of her. Maggie listened to the Padre saying prayers in Latin like the ones in Mass. She could tell he was getting tired too—his cross had been trying to droop down for a long time. The Padre's feet were covered in dust and there was justice in this.

Finally everyone stopped along the side of the road where there were some rocks. They sat down and took out something to eat. Some of the men had been carrying the tortillas wrapped in a cloth under their hats. Mariana had a bottle of water to drink. She went with Maggie a little ways behind a big rock to pee. Maggie stood guard for her mother and then she looked where their puddles should have been and there was nothing left but a wet spot; it had already sunk into the ground. When Maggie peed, she got some on her leg and it burned from the sun. Her hair was all sweaty when she took her scarf off but it felt good in the breeze. The procession got ready to move again. The kids had just started to look and smile shyly at each other. Not too big or too long smiles in case someone was looking and thought they were having fun on this sacred walk. So they did it quickly and then looked down. Soon they would have been running after each other, but that was not allowed today. It would come later after the prayers were finished.

So they were walking again. The desert seemed to be turning as they walked. There were many mesquite and chollas everywhere. After each step everything looked alike but different at the same time. Maggie tried to get close to Bale. When he saw her, the fingers of one hand wriggled at her behind his back. But he pretended not to see her. His mother was right next to him and the priest didn't miss anything either.

This walk was full of sorrow like when they prayed for dead people at Nina's house. When everyone was in black and they stayed on their knees for hours and it was in the sala that was never opened except for celebrations and for death. The living room was always kept apart. It was that way now. Nobody was just talking. They were praying for the dead in the family. Praying and feeling things, maybe even wishing the dead weren't dead though that was not the point of this. Maggie squinted her eyes to see where the sun was and sneaked a look at Mama. Mariana's face was sad and her hands kept turning the beads. Maggie thought she must be thinking about her father, Maggie's real father. But the child didn't think about him. She didn't remember him. She felt the dust on her feet. She thought of hunting for chucata at the end of the summer. She thought of gathering bellota in between the summer rains, and the way the sage smelled afterward that made her look all the way to the mountains, blue mountains. She didn't know what she was looking for at times like that. She was just thinking, My father is not here, he has never been here, I don't smell him in the sage. That's why my father is not here. She tried to think of him walking around in these hills before her but she couldn't imagine it because the sage was empty of him. There was only her. A skinny ugly little girl with strange yellow hair like no one else's.

She walked and walked. The Padre and the altar boys were doing something again. They started praying out loud, this time in Spanish so everyone could understand and answer back. The Padre said one thing and the people said something else and then they started over again. "*Santa Maria, Madre de Dios, llena tu eres de gracia...* Hail Mary, full of grace," and then Maggie got lost in something about her "front" and she didn't know what it meant and then everybody said, "Pray for us now and at the hour of our death," and why did they have to bring in dying all the time? The incense was swinging and there was a lot of making the sign of the cross, little crosses on the forehead and the chest and then a big one. Nobody looked at the children to see if they were doing it right; they followed as best they could, and then they were walking faster. Maggie saw over the tops of the mesquites something white. And then they changed direction and way ahead of them there was a white cross. It was far away but they were walking straight at it. The people in front were already beginning to climb the hill which was so steep they sort of stumbled, and those coming behind bumped into them and then everybody slowed down. They trudged one step at a time in the dust. The children got thirstier but there was no use asking for anything because nobody was stopping. There was barrel cactus along the hillside and when they got higher up they could see cottonwoods on the other side of the fields and the leaves shimmering with silver. Now they could feel the breezes. Suddenly they were at the top of the hill by the cave where Mary was with her Son; the iron gates had been opened and pushed way over to the side. Many were tying colored ribbons to the bars. The women were cleaning the dust away from the floor of the grotto with their pañuelos. Maggie and Mariana were next in line and just ahead of them was a señora from El Barrio Central, the one from the bakery where they made the greatest Pan de Huevo. But now she was ready to have a baby and her husband helped her get up from kneeling, reaching for her with long arms and Maggie saw his clean shirt had the cuffs folded back and buttoned over the wrists because the sleeves were too long. But he put his arm around la señora protectively and smiled at Maggie too. She wished he were at home with them instead of Frank. She smiled back shyly but he was already looking away and Mariana was pulling at her hand. She found a waxed string and lit the end of it and then lit the candles Mariana placed as close to Mary and Jesus as she could. She was praying, not looking at Maggie, and there was nothing for her to do but to look at *them*. Jesus's hand was falling on the ground and there was a big gash in it and His stomach was caved in. His eyes were half open and she could see His teeth inside His open mouth. She felt afraid. She didn't know what to do while Mariana was praying, and Mary was so open—there were large tears on her face the same color as her skin. She had unwrapped her Son so all could see His wounds. She held her arms open showing them her Son. Maggie's throat was tight. She didn't know why she wanted to cry. She wouldn't cry here because there was no place to hide and anyway, nobody cried in front of these statues. She didn't want to look anymore. She looked at Jesus's feet but His bare uncovered feet, so gentle...and she pulled at Mariana who did not protest and then it was over and they were almost running down the hill.

The smells of carne asada and beans cooking under the ramadas brought them to the big pots of food. It was a relief to feel hunger and thirst and to want the company of all the other people. Now it was like a celebration. Maybe it was like after someone had been buried; then everybody ate and laughed to remember their own bodies still alive. Maggie wandered around. She saw an Indio taking a huge bite from one end of a fat burrito; a bunch of chili beans squeezed out and he caught them with his fingers and pushed them back into his mouth. Other people were eating tamales right from the husk, and coffee was steaming from a can on the fire. A little boy, smaller than Maggie, was eating a tortilla running with honey, so now she started looking for Mariana and heard her nina calling her. She ate everything they were eating: lechuga and tamale and beans and café with sugar. When she was done the sun did not feel so hot anymore, so she went around seeing what there was to do and she found Bale playing around the crosses.

"My mother made me," he said, "she talked to the priest behind my back." They walked around looking at the graves with pink and blue and yellow crosses and ribbons on them. "It's only for three weeks," he continued, "and sometimes when nobody's looking, we swipe wine from the bottle the priests keep in the closet. So being an altar boy is not bad."

"Aren't you afraid God will punish you?" asked Maggie.

"I'm not afraid of God," said Bale. They found a little baby's grave hung with tinsel and Christmas balls. Then it was getting dark and they played hide-and-go-seek with the kids from El Barrio Central. La Milpa played against the Barrio with the rancherías on their side. When it was too dark to find anybody, and it was getting scary, Maggie started looking for Mariana. People were around the fires but Maggie was too hot and she went to find the water bucket, turning the big cup around to a different side like Grandmother showed her. The water tasted nice and cold and while she was drinking she saw the stars. A big star blinking at her. There were a lot of smaller stars over the mountains, where she lived, that she didn't notice at first. A spread of red over the little black peaks was still standing out against the sky. She always felt this way, like there was some place she wanted to go. Or maybe she had already been there inside the little peaks or behind the red sky. She remembered something but didn't know what or who. Or when. But she remembered someone who felt the night breeze blowing against her throat. Someone in the middle of a desert big enough for rocky hills and mountains. And miles and miles of cactus and mesquites and dried-up pieces of wood and stickers and looking at the sloping-up mountains turning into rocky peaks. And yellow clouds falling back into a sky that never ends all the way to the back of nothing....

And then she could breathe again and it was time to run back and find everybody.

Chapter 7

▲

Maggie was playing by herself under the tamarack tree. She counted twigs, making them all the same size, made many little houses, big ones and small ones with slanted roofs and peaked roofs where no one lived. She cleared paths among the dry tamarack needles, making roads go farther away. She made a playground in case someone came. She played until she got tired of it. Then she lay on the ground looking up at the cold grey sky, at the high clouds mushrooming up from behind the mountains. She imagined she could hear the rio, a low wet sound, but she did not want to walk all the way to the river.

Without making noise, she looked carefully through a crack in the door of the shack. Saw *her* sewing on a bit of white cloth. Colored pictures, little bits of thread, red and yellow, blue, purple. Her own fingers were too rough—the thread would catch on them. Or she pulled the thread too tightly, breaking it and making the picture wrinkle up. Not like she who had fine sensitive fingers, a musician's fingers, and soft waving hair, eyes so very light brown like butterfly's wings, not like her own hard dark eyes.

She watched her mama smooth the embroidery, her slim fingers and long nails touching the cloth. She saw her own hand on the door, the large square fist her hand made. She tore her hand away from the door jumping like a startled animal.

She ran around the back of the house, stood staring at the woodpile and then got the axe from the porch. She would chop wood. That was what her big rough hands were good for. She would do this for her beautiful mama whose hands were too fine for chopping wood. She swung the man-sized axe. Brought it down hard on the big piece of wood placed across another piece the way she had seen men do it. Her shoulders felt the weight of the axe and the blow to the wood and it felt good. She remembered to watch where her toes were placed, also the way she had seen men do it.

She chopped and piled the kindling and the big wood in separate piles making them neat. She worked not caring how cold it was. She swung the axe above her head splitting the wood open to its yellow center, smelling the fresh wood smell and liking the wood chips that collected at her feet. When she had a big pile of logs she put away the axe. She piled the wood inside the porch and covered the remaining wood with a tarp. She gathered a big armful of kindling and went inside. She went to the stove. She could tell from being in the room it would be cold. She looked in her mother's room, saw her lying down with eyes closed. She tiptoed away, lit some newspaper carefully, added kindling and opened the vent to let the smoke out. Soon the fire was going strong so she lowered the vent and got the heavy irons, placing them on top of the stove.

She would iron for her mother. She would work hard for her. She opened the ironing board, struggling to make it stand up. She got some laundry and sprinkled each piece with water at the sink. Then she wrapped it all up to soak while the irons got hot. She ironed each shirt carefully the way her nina had taught her. First the collar, then the back, the sleeves and lastly the two fronts. She put them on hangers, careful not to make a single wrinkle. She ironed the pañuelos last, enjoying the simplicity of each square piece of cloth. She was putting away the ironing board when she saw her mother standing in the doorway, one hand nervously smoothing back her hair.

"*Por qué quemas leña en la estufa?* Why are you burning wood in the stove?" she asked. "He is going to be angry."

"*A mí no me hace.* It doesn't bother me. Who cares what he thinks?" It wasn't what Maggie had wanted to say. "I did the ironing for you..." she started to say but seeing Mariana's face pinch up with fear made her mad. "Mama, it was freezing in here." But Mariana was looking out the window, searching in both directions and not listening to her.

"If he's coming, I'm going over to Grandmother's."

"You know he doesn't want you to be going over there." Mariana seemed frightened.

"Why not? She likes it when I'm there."

"She'd never tell *you* the truth!" His heavy voice came from behind her. Maggie turned around but refused to show she was scared.

"She would so tell me the truth. She never lies," Maggie stated more bravely than she felt. "And she likes it and I'm going!"

He stared at her with hard unreadable eyes and Mariana said quickly, "You must obey your father."

"He didn't say I couldn't and I'm going." She made a rush for the bedroom, planning to run out the back door, but his large heavy hand landed on her shoulder.

"Who do you think you're talking to like that?" His grip on her shoulder started to tighten, she felt the cloth pull tight, but she wriggled free and dashed with real fear through the door. She plunged outside, surprised he was not coming after her, but she heard his threatening voice as she swung open the gate.

"You have to come back sometime and I'll get you then!" The last thing she heard was her mother's voice. She hesitated. For a dizzying moment she thought he was sneaking out the back to get her before she ran through the gate. But she didn't see him as she ran along the fence heading for the road.

She was sorry to leave her mama there alone. And she had run out without her sweater; the cold hit her over-heated body with a shock. She thought of the shirts she had hung so carefully on their hangers, *his* shirts, and she began to cry wishing she could be warm with her mother by the fire. The fire *she* had made. She had done it all for her, not him. And now Mariana would suffer because she had left, and *he* would enjoy it all, putting his big stinking feet up on the stove to get warm.

She ran as fast as she could down the dirt road. Her throat was dry and she was panting hard by the time she started across the bridge to La Milpa. She saw Bale and some other kids she knew playing on the bridge but she didn't want them to see her crying, so she didn't stop. She ran along the river to El Barrio Central. She had run herself out when it began to rain. It was a cold fine rain and she walked as fast as she could while holding her blouse together at the throat. The low adobe houses of the Barrio were silent in the rain and distant with their heavy wooden doors shut tight. She started to pass Cien Milla, changed her mind and cut up to the high ground and the trail through the mesquite. She wanted to stop and pick up a few sticks for Grandmother's fire the way she always did but she was too tired and too frightened.

She didn't meet anyone. It was supper time now and she smelled cooking as she ran down the other side of Cien Milla towards Las Rancherías Chiquitas near the railroad tracks.

She saw Grandmother's tub and washboard leaning against the fence. Her comal was empty of ashes—she must have cleaned it out, saving the ashes in a coffee can for the flowers. Maggie undid the piece of wire that fastened the gate shut, let herself in and tied it up again. She was shaking when she knocked loudly on the wooden door. She heard the old woman open the inner door and make her way along the wall in the dark.

"*Yo soy.* It's me," she called out.

"*Ay eres tu, m'hija?* Oh, it's you, my daughter?" Grandmother unlocked the door and peered out from under the black tapalo she wore summer and winter. Her grey eyes were impersonal but her voice was caring and warm. In the dark shadows of the entranceway, she suddenly appeared very old to Maggie and a sudden apprehension of death came to her. Before she could say anything in the voice she had planned, she started to cry.

"What is wrong?" Grandmother's voice was strong. "Did the ox spank you?" Maggie started to laugh at the same time she was crying. Grandmother felt her forehead, bringing her in towards the stove. She sat Maggie down in her special chair by the fire and went to replace the rags against the door to keep out the drafts. Maggie rubbed her head it hurt so much. Grandmother came back. "And why are you going alone in the cold then?" She sounded angry and made Maggie take her wet shoes off giving her a pair of cotton stockings to put on her feet.

Maggie smelled posol cooking on the stove but instead of being hungry it made her want to throw up. At last Grandmother came with her jar of ointment, rubbed it all over Maggie's forehead and tied her head tightly with a rag. It was not her way to comfort with words but Maggie was comforted as Grandmother put her into the big bed.

"He said you were a...a bad woman," Maggie cried tearfully.

"And what does he know? Of my life and of you he knows nothing and he will never know."

Hija, algunas veces pasa algo y se supone que todo fue claro, pero ya después sale que fue completamente al revés de lo que pensamos al principio. Así fue la primera vez que vi de carne y hueso al que se llama El Tejano.

Daughter, sometimes something happens and we suppose that everything was clear, but then later it turns out that things were completely different from what we thought at first. That's how it was the first time I saw in flesh and bone the one called The Texan.

Grandmother told me it was when the grass was high in late summer that she saw him. The rabbits were standing up smelling the breeze. The air carried the smell of water. And it was in looking down from the heavens and towards the hills that she saw someone.

He came walking through the grass that wiped its tall wet ends against his knees. The clouds hung above his head. "Lo vi todo en blanco. I saw him all in white. He looked so fine in his outfit," Grandmother said. "'Where did you come from?' I asked him. 'I don't see your horse anywhere.'

"'O, para allá está, dentro de las lomitas. Oh, it's over there, between the hills,' he said, gesturing back the way he had come.

"That's when I noticed that he spoke with the voice in his nose, the way Texans talk," she said. "And I saw how fine the bridge of his nose was." Grandmother pinched her fingers together to show me how thin the bridge of his nose was. "And I looked down at his feet," she said. "I saw that his feet were small and his boots of beautiful white leather.

'Bueno, it looks like it's going to rain,' I told him, looking up at the gathering clouds.

"'Yes, it looks like it,' he said."

She looked out at the hediondilla, at the bellota and the piles of wood she was gathering, then at the tent where the baby was sleeping. The meadow they were in was shielded to the west and to the east by rounded hills; to the north was the Pass through which they'd come. And to the south, pinion trees dotted the slope in ever-thickening branches until they disappeared into low cloud.

The wind gusted suddenly bringing the first drops of rain. She saw the wind strike his slender body, stirring the fringe on his white shirt. Then she turned to the tent, saying that she was going to cover up the baby.

"I turned to cover you, hija," Grandmother told me, "and when I looked back, I didn't see him anymore." But where did he go? she asked herself. And then very finely the rain began to fall. But how can I not see him? The cowboy with blue eyes? The one I was talking to? Seeing all at the same time the desert high country, the pinions falling over with fruit and the fast-moving storm cloud. And then they were in the midst of the rain and she wrapped the canvas around them leaving only a crack to look out from.

The rain came down finely, finely, without lightning, as if the clouds were merely brushing across the face of the earth. Then thunder cracked loudly in her ears. She sat *inside the canvas cover while large drops pelted them from every side. After long moments of heavy rain, the thunder began to sound from farther away and the rain to slacken. She looked out at the gently sloping meadow and the pinion trees and down at the child she held in her arms. And recalling the face of the visitor, she was no longer sure of what she had seen, or rather, if it was possible.*

Like a drawing layer by layer the face took form. The impossible eyes. One of them open and unblinking in the light. Like the eye of a rattlesnake perpetually facing the brightness of the sun, the pupil a slit in the golden circle of the eye almost seeming to cast its own shadow. The other eye dark and liquid spilling over in tears that never fall against the cheek. And deep in its depths the laughter, the joy. "And now I am not even sure if it was the face of a man or a woman I saw," Grandmother told me.

Maggie opened her eyes and saw Grandmother sitting in front of the stove, her hands on her stick. She had made the fire warmer, using more of the small pile of precious sticks. Maggie vowed that tomorrow she would go out into the chaparral and find Grandmother the biggest pile of lenia and bring it to her. Tomorrow when she woke up her headache would be gone.

"Grandmother," Maggie said sleepily, "are you going to die?" Grandmother turned to her. "Everything ends, mi hija, but I will not die until you are grown." Maggie closed her eyes, satisfied. Grandmother continued to sit by the fire. She was thinking about another evening, another storm on the way....

The Great White Horse moves without effort always inside the calm center of the storm. Driven by the fury of the wind, dark tumultuous clouds grow. And the setting sun is caught by galloping cloud so the sky and earth are illuminated by blood.

It is a finely built person who rides the Great White Horse. Fine of build, fine of feature, fine of hands and feet. Boots of white leather rest gently against the great heaving sides of the horse. As the horse enters the darkening canyon, the rider's shirt strikes light; the horse's hooves strike rock; but they ride the edge without sound. They move inside shadows cast by the approaching storm. It is not clear if the white horse and its rider are really there; if they are of flesh and blood. They are more like the white thickening cloud against the rough walls of the canyon rising upwards. More like the deep magnetic energy that builds a storm. They are black drops of rain falling tenderly the long sweeping distance to the desert floor. They make the streaming black and white waters appear and disappear as they fall. They are the bridge between day and night and life and death. At last it seems as though the rider and the Great White Horse are moving beyond Adela Sewa's vision. She hears the wind beat against her shelter with all the force of the angry skies and the cry of a terrible sorrow. The wind hurls itself from the head of a giant saguaro and is flung back to the heavens by the twisted fingers of ironwood. She wakes with the rustling of pinion trees. A smell of sage is strong. Another gust of wind shakes the shelter and she immediately comes fully awake listening intently for any other sound. Hearing nothing she moves quickly to search in the basket beside her, feeling inside the small bundle for the warmth of life. Satisfied, Adela Sewa turns the lamp higher, casting her own face into relief: the broad forehead, the piercing grey eyes. Her motions are quick and determined, not affected by fatigue or sadness. She encourages the glowing embers, making a small fire to warm milk in a can. The tiny infant, Margarita, looks at her with wide open eyes as she pries open her mouth with a finger and squeezes a few drops of milk in from the corner of a rag. The baby sucks on the cloth making tiny sounds. Again and again Adela Sewa wets the bit of rag with milk and gives it to the child. Then it is quiet again. The clear silvery radiance of the moon touches the edge of the bundle and the tiny face wrapped within. The woman makes a cloth barrier so the moon cannot eat the child's face. She drifts towards sleep once more, waiting without thought for the hoofbeats she knows will come. The movement against the canvas, the impossible shadows behind the lamplight waking her so she can feed the baby and keep her alive.

While Adela Sewa sleeps the rain falls drop by drop between grains of sand, seeping down among hard clean rock among roots growing finer and finer until the eye cannot see nor the mind comprehend the thirst.

Grandmother sat before the fire finding in the flames memories of those other nights. Then she went about checking the doors, tapping the rags snugly into the cracks with the tip of her stick. She got into bed beside the sleeping child, murmuring to herself, "I suppose I made her live just so the ox could mistreat her!" In answer to her words the wind shook the house. Beyond the chaparral and high on a rocky ledge, a coyote walked stiff-legged to the mouth of her cave and stood with lowered outstretched head, staring out at last light and the rain falling coldly against her rocky ledge. Faint shadows of the hillsides curving away and indistinct forms of cactus and mesquite were all the coyote could see. The small creatures of the desert would not venture far from their burrows tonight. There would be no hunting. She licked her snout, made a half barking sound in her throat that ended in a soft whine of hunger and returned to her burrow. But she would not sleep. She lay with her nose on her tail looking out at the grey light. Her sensitive nose picked up the scent of the cold dirt beneath her body, the wet green smell of sage and the thick musky smell of resin from the chapperal. From far away, the smell of Grandmother's posol was lifted by the winds. The coyote sniffed hopefully and then resigned to hunger put her nose down and lay with shining eyes.

In Cien Milla, a shonte emerged from her twig nest in the thorny arms of a cholla. She danced around and then re-entered her nest. She too stared out for long moments at the impenetrable rain before puffing out her feathers. Settling them with her beak she succumbed to the limitations of the storm.

Grandmother's eyes sprung open one last time, her grey eyes were flashing and her voice iron. "I suppose!" she said aloud, reaching for her stick and thumping it against the floor for emphasis. And she grinned at the darkness.

Chapter 8

▲

"No me quiero ir, Abuelita. I don't want to go back, Grandmother. Why do I have to?"

"No dejes que te asuste. Don't let him scare you,"
Grandmother ordered. Maggie *was* afraid.

"But why can't I live here?"

"While your mama lives, you have to stand it."

"She doesn't listen to me, and she lets him do whatever
he wants..."

"He won't do anything to you today. And the day will
come when all that he has done will pile up on him."

"I'll go because I love you more than anybody." Maggie
threw her arms around the old woman, pushing her off
balance.

"Now go, go," she said sternly. "You must make yourself into a woman quickly as you can, that's all."

"You said you'd live until I grew up," Maggie teased,
still not comprehending, "so I don't want to hurry up."

"Go now." Grandmother pushed her towards the door. "I have things I must do." As Maggie left, Grandmother was sweeping her altar with a palm branch she used only for that purpose.

Maggie went with her stomach full of warm posol and her spirits lifted. She sniffed the desert air. The sky had cleared overnight. Although it was early afternoon, there was still dew on the ground in places the sun had not touched. Maggie shivered but her body benefited from the brisk walk. She was whistling by the time she reached home. She had enjoyed walking and talking to the sparrows that took flight and settled as she passed. She had forgotten the sorrows of the day before, but when her hand touched the gate she remembered and was afraid. Before she could decide what to do, Frank's voice rang out and she saw him sitting on the woodpile. He had been watching her come up the road.

"Come here. I want to show you something," he called. She walked towards him slowly but he did not seem angry. He waved her over. He opened a small wooden box and took out a shiny pistol. He put the gun into her hands. "Don't tell anybody," he said. Her fingers fell into place around the butt, reaching for the trigger. He seemed satisfied by the way the gun fit her hand and he showed her how to stand and take aim; how to adjust for the recoil. Then he got shells to show her how they went into the chamber and helped her brace for the first shots.

She fired at the target he had set up without questioning these events. She did what he told her to do, getting used to the gun, the strange feel of the cold blue steel. She had watched him cleaning his guns before and spreading them out on a piece of red cloth, arranging them until they suited him. She had seen him oiling and cleaning and polishing, but he had never invited her to touch anything.

"This is a Peacemaker," he was saying. "A Colt .41 six shot. It's easier for you to hold because of the shorter barrel. Feel the weight of it and balance it in your hand." She was surprised: he wasn't telling her to run in the house and put on a dress. He didn't seem to care that she was a girl.

"This is what the cowboys used. It was made in 1873. It's heavy but you'll get used to it."

"Is it mine?" she dared to ask.

"No. It's for learning. But if you do good, when you're older we'll see."

"Will we go shoot in the desert?"

"For that you'll need a rifle." He took the gun from her hand and wiped the barrel with a cloth. "We'll see how you do with this first. I want you to fire the rest of these shells. But do it the way I told you because they cost money."

She handled the Colt carefully while he watched intently. For the first time she wasn't afraid of him. They were not hating each other. They were two strangers in common admiration of the task of learning. She leaned her shooting shoulder against the tree trunk for support and then gradually stood free of it, letting her breath out slowly and then holding it and gently squeezing the trigger. She was still afraid of the recoil, but learned not to anticipate it and to brace her feet. Her arms and legs were beginning to shake when he told her to stop. She was dumb from the noise and could not smell anything but gunpowder.

"Look it!" He showed her the target. One hole was near the center. "If you keep up this way and practice, you'll be good."

"I want to show Mama!"

"Not until you've cleaned the gun." She rested while he got the cleaning things ready. She was learning to shoot. Two doves flew overhead. She saw them clearly, looking at the world more closely, more carefully. Her big hands and strong legs were good for something. First for chopping wood, and now this too.

Frank went over each step in cleaning and then made her do it. "Next time you'll do it by yourself," he warned. So she very carefully worked the hot soapy water back and forth in the bore with a long brush. Then she wiped the barrel with a piece of flannel. Next she applied some oil to the metal she had just cleaned, but not too much. He said they wouldn't take the lock off this time because it had just been cleaned. Finally, he showed her how to put the Colt away carefully in its little box. "You never just leave it wrapped up," he said, "because it'll get wet inside the cloth and start to rust." At last she was free to run inside and show Mariana the target with the shots she had made. Mariana smiled faintly but didn't say anything. Maggie was too excited to notice her mother's sadness or the slow way she moved about the room getting supper ready.

When Frank came in she bravely addressed him and asked when she could practice again. "Soon," was all he would say. But it was enough. Maggie ate in a hurry. "Can I go to Grandmother's? I want to show her my shooting," she said proudly.

"Margarita..." Mariana began, but Frank interrupted, "Sure, go tell the old lady how I'm teaching you."

On her way, Maggie shouted to the boys hanging out at the bridge, "I'm learning to shoot a gun!" She barely stopped long enough to show them the target. "That's my bullet." She stuck her finger through the hole near the center and ran on. She lingered to gather a few sticks in Cien Milla to add to what she had gathered that morning and then hurried through the desert in the direction of the railroad tracks.

Grandmother was outside looking over the effect of the rain on her plants. She peered closely at the target Maggie held up to her. *"Que no te pego?* Didn't he spank you?" she asked in mock sternness.

"Ni estaba enojado. He wasn't even mad. And then he showed me how to shoot and it's going to be mine when I'm bigger—it's a gun like the cowboys had!" Maggie stopped talking and Grandmother grunted, "Just be careful and don't try to shoot animals. They live like us."

"Don't worry, Grandmother. I'll never hurt anything, not even the trees."

"Then you must figure out what it's for." Grandmother was smiling but her tone was serious. "So you made up?" she asked in a lighter voice.

"I'll still hate him if he's mean to us, but I'm glad he showed me something." Maggie was skipping about like a happy little girl. Not bent over like an old woman like me, Grandmother thought. "Come with me," she said to Maggie. She made the child wipe the altar with the palm branch and place her hands for a moment on the stone before lighting a candle. The one she lit the candle in front of was a small black statue with bits of turquoise for eyes.

"Who is that, Grandmother?" Maggie asked.

"We cannot sound her name in this world, but she is called The Dark One. She comes from far away. She cares for the desert and for woman."

"How come I didn't see her in church?"

"Her you won't see in the church."

"How come?"

"Because she obeys only woman."

"But why does she have teeth, Grandmother?"

"To bite off a goat's head," said Grandmother. But she didn't say it out loud, only to herself. To Maggie she said, "Tomorrow you will come with me."

"I will?"

"Yes. We will look for herbs. We will walk a long ways and I am old. Now be quiet. Spirits cannot be heard when we talk too much. We will sit outside a little and wait for the sun to go out."

"I have to go back before it gets too dark," Maggie said reluctantly. She liked to watch it get dark the best.

"Then I will walk a little ways with you," said Grandmother. Maggie always wanted to walk with Grandmother, even a short ways, because she was so happy just to walk slowly looking at everything together. They walked in silence this evening until they reached Cien Milla. Maggie had been looking at the mountains.

"I wish we could go up into the mountains, the ones you know," she said.

"The light ahead of us, and we behind. Tomorrow we'll go."

Maggie kept turning around to wave as long as she could still see Grandmother who stood with her back to the desert, leaning on her stick. She lifted her tapalo with one hand and covered her head more firmly. The black cotton skirt she wore reached to her ankles; her shirt, one of many "pintitos" of grey and white, fit over her wide hips. The rebozo over her shoulders was a deep red like a smear of ochre in the muted light. Even in this fading light, Maggie could see and feel the strength and magnetism of her eyes. Distance was nothing. Finally the mesquite was too high to see anymore and Maggie shouted a last goodbye. Grandmother raised her stick high in answer and Maggie turned and ran down the well-worn trail through Cien Milla.

The doves were roosting, their sound the softest most peaceful loving sound she knew. Her heart filled with happiness. The few clouds still in the west were red when she broke out of Cien Milla and started on the dirt road around Los Quates. To the east La Madre was a creamy blue and above her the sky was turning purple. Maggie liked facing east when she was coming back from Grandmother's. She felt love and protection from the mountain; assured of a place in the world. And a place after death in the shadow of its face. Maggie's life and her world were known and complete.

El Cuento:

Antes de que llegaran los Jesuitas vivíamos libres en el monte, pero ya después dejamos las rancherías y vivimos en pueblos. Allí en uno de ellos cerca del río Yaqui nací yo. Al principio tuvimos jefes, pero después los mejicanos se pusieron muy fuertes. Un día vinieron los soldados y se llevaron a mis hermanos que quedaban porque decían que ayudaban a los Yaquis que estaban en guerra. Colgaron a mis hermanos de una piocha y tiraron los cuerpos en medio del camino para ver quién los iba a levantar. Entonces vinieron a llevarse a las mujeres. Nos mandaron a Yucatán a trabajar las minas de plata. No volví a ver a mi mamá ni a mi hermana, pero allí murieron. Cuando a los muchos años me vine para Sonora, ya no había alma que me conociera. Por todo eso, para mí ya no existe Mejico.

Adela Sewa Kome'ela
n. 1870, Potam, Sonora, Mejico
m. 1958, El Pueblo, Arizona, E.U.A.

The Story:

Before the Jesuits came, we lived freely on the plains. But after that we left the rancherías and lived in villages. In one of them I was born near the Yaqui river. In the beginning we had leaders, but then the Mexicans grew in strength. One day the soldiers came and took my brothers who were left because it was said they helped the Yaquis who were making war against them. They hung my brothers from a tree and threw the bodies in the middle of the road to see who would come to lift them up. Then they came to take the women. They sent us to Yucatan to work in the silver mines. I never saw my mother or my sister again, but they died there. When I came back to Sonora after many years, no one knew me. Because of all this, for me, Mexico no longer exists.

Adela Sewa Kome'ela
b. 1870, Potam, Sonora, Mexico
d. 1958, El Pueblo, Arizona, U.S.A.

Chapter 9

▲

"*Abuelita, porqué no te quedastes en Mejico?* Grandmother, how come you didn't stay in Mexico?" They were picking jojoba in the chaparral, Grandmother pointing out the mature beans on their short stout bushes.

"*Para qué?* What for?" She reached for a bean, her strong fingers twisting it out of its shell.

"To be with your people."

"They put me out because I had a son by a Spaniard."

"But what about here? How come you didn't live in the village with the other Yaquis?"

"Because they are in the church too much like the Mexicans. But also I like to have my own house. That way I don't put myself in with the Mexicans or with the Yaquis or the Americans."

Maggie's heart thumped hearing those words. "But I'm all of those things! I'm nothing but a bowl full of cotton," she said, lips trembling.

Grandmother said nothing. She looked out over the dark green and sienna of the creosote bushes, at the bright yellow blossoms traveling up the desert slopes. Each plant was growing with complete knowledge of itself yearning only to be what it was. She placed the jojoba beans in the paper bag and walked on to the next plant. They grew in small groupings along the west side of the trail.

"I'm going to show you how to cure jojoba so you can put it on your lashes. You will see how beautiful they will become."

"How can I be pretty with this hair?" Yanking at the coarse cowlicks of yellow hair, Maggie continued, "and I don't even have any lashes. All I have are these slanted eyes."

"Be quiet, little one," Grandmother said, not unkindly. "Some day you will gain from all the different kinds of blood you have. One day you will understand."

"I want to be like you, Grandmother, all one thing! And I'm not even pretty like my mama. I'm ugly!" She was ready to cry but knew that Grandmother did not like displays of emotion for frivolous reasons.

"Who told you that?"

"*He* says it all the time. And its true I don't look like Mama. She's so beautiful and I don't even have curly hair."

"Your mama is French and Spanish. And don't pay attention to that man. He is not your father. He was tall like you. And he had the same eyes."

"Why didn't he ever come here?"

"Because he died very young and your mama's family threw her out. Then she came over here and looked for me. She fell very ill. You were only a few days old so you would not have lived without her."

"Is that when you took care of me, Grandmother? But why did they throw my mama from the house?"

"For the same reason the same kind of people took my son away and I left your grandfather's land—because they had blue blood, and your papa, however much they didn't want it, had the blood of a Yaqui. While I was there they could not deny it. And then later, when he was dead, they wanted to punish your mama for going with him. You see, always trying to make everything and everyone the same is not so worthwhile."

But Maggie had gone from wanting to cry to wanting to get even. "Why did he have to die?" She kicked at the roots of the jojoba.

"Don't harm the plants!" Grandmother pulled Maggie away. "Everything dies, only some before others. And then," she continued, "that gringo came out and your mama wanted to marry him."

"But why?"

"Because at first he was like sugar and she believed it."

"But why doesn't she get a divorce?"

Grandmother picked jojoba for a while in silence, deciding what to say. "Your mama has never been strong," she said at last. "One must have the opportunity not only to suffer but to become strong. And he has her tied up."

"Nobody's ever going to do that to me!" Maggie said, marching around.

"You are going to step on the plants I tell you! Sit down if you can't work." Grandmother took the bag from Maggie's hands and worked at the same steady pace while Maggie sat on some large rocks and scratched at the sandy quartz with her fingernails. Specks of mica shone in the sunlight.

"Grandmother, where do I get this hair from?"

"Your grandfather's people were very light. He came from the north of Spain. He had black hair, but blue eyes. I think in his family there were some like you. But now, that's enough talking."

Maggie knew there would be no more conversation now. Grandmother had spoken more than usual. Maggie wished she could be like her and go days without speaking. But she always sang to the cactus and shouted at the coyotes for no reason. And at school she talked more than all the boys—the girls didn't count because she couldn't sit down with them long enough to find out.

"Grandmother, I'm going to pick some sage." She always wanted to walk among the sage. It always smelled like the desert right after a rain, even after sitting in a jar for a long time. She could crush it between her fingers and bring the smell of the rain back again. That was the last thing she did before going to sleep every night: crush a few of the tiny tough leaves between her fingers and lift them to her face. Everything in the desert is tough and lasts a long time, she thought, looking around. A slight movement made her peer ahead. She saw a young coyote, a female by its build, pass on the trail going east. The coyote, her long ears standing straight up, had her head turned towards Maggie as she passed; her large intelligent eyes registered neither fear nor hostility. The coyote put her nose to the ground and continued on her way. Maggie saw the tawny grey of her coat disappear quickly downslope. Hunting jackrabbit, she thought. The jacks were everywhere this spring, even Nina had caught two in her trap and made conejo con chile. Maggie had sucked the meat from the delicate bones like everyone else, though she did not like to see them killed. "I know how you feel," she called after the departing coyote.

When she had snapped off enough branches of sage to please herself, she went back to Grandmother who was sitting on a rock in the shade of a mesquite. She had taken a white pañuelo from her pocket. Wrapped inside were some tortillas and pieces of jerky.

"I saw a coyote," Maggie began. Grandmother did not answer so Maggie composed herself and ate the food in silence. Grandmother wiped the lip of the water jar with her pañuelo and handed it over. Maggie drank, wiped the lip and handed it back. Grandmother placed the jar in the shade.

The rains that came in early spring were over. There were no more quelites and the sun was hot by midday. Grandmother found a place to lie down and rest until the hottest part of the day was past. Maggie looked for a place for herself and chose a large mesquite a little way up the slope behind them. There was a path of clear earth and the branches of the mesquite hung above it loaded with young bean pods. The branches swayed in the breeze making the area beneath it cool.

The afternoon passed slowly. Maggie made little houses out of rocks and knocked them down again. At times she paused in her play to gaze out at the chaparral. She could see Grandmother wrapped in her rebozo lying very still beside the rocks. A blue haze hung along the foothills to the east. Closer by, the twin peaks of Los Quates rose into the sky. She could see movement sometimes on the lower slopes—kids from La Milpa playing cowboys and Indians or World War Two. She was not high enough to see, but she knew that at this time of day the men would be at home en la siesta. Later on when it was cooler they would return to the fields to hoe among the new squash, corn and watermelon plants. She remembered Bale, and his little brother Eddie, whom they both had to tug along by his arms so he wouldn't step on the vines, hanging around the men when they went out to test the first melons. Whoever was there got to taste a piece held out to them on the edge of a sharp knife. Eddie slurped on his piece, gnawing on the rind long after there was no more red left; they had to take it away from him so he wouldn't get a stomachache. Maggie laughed thinking about it. Then she saw Grandmother moving and ran down to her in a shower of rocks.

"Don't make dust." Grandmother waved her tapalo to clear the air. Maggie helped her sit up, sitting beside her while she braided her loose hair. She rinsed her mouth with water and after spitting, wiped her face with a damp pañuelo.

"Are we going to pick some more?"

"No, we have enough."

Maggie put all the jojoba beans together in one bag, put the water jug on top of them and squeezed the bag shut so she could carry it with one hand. Grandmother did not seem ready to go yet, so she waited. Then Grandmother spoke: *"Te voy a decir una cosa.* I am going to tell you something," she began. "Do you see over there the mountain we call La Madre?"

"Yes."

"When I am ready to die, that is where I will come."

"What do you mean, Grandmother?" A tremor of fear went through Maggie. Grandmother reached for her hand and held it in a very strong grip.

"Do not be afraid. I want to go before the world changes too much." Maggie did not know what she meant. She thought everything was the same.

"The world will change a lot. I could not live then like I must. The coyotes and the rabbit will go too. Right now, horita, they are looking for a way to go to La Madre. The corn and the melons will not grow at the feet of Los Quates anymore. *No se como,* I don't know how, but all of La Milpa will be gone."

"How can the corn not grow anymore, Grandmother?"

"The earth is tired, used up. She must rest. For this the gringos have come. The day will come soon when nothing will grow there anymore. It will become desert too.

The gringos will still use it for something," she added. "But what I want to tell you is this: when the time comes, I will come to La Madre. I will come to her and I will not return."

"But Grandmother," Maggie swallowed hard, "aren't you going to be buried in the cemetery?"

Grandmother spit. "I do not need the church to say what piece of ground is blessed. Do you think they are going to put me in a hole? No! In the arms of La Madre I go. I have my place ready. I will cover the mouth with rocks and there I will stay."

"But what if the animals get you?"

"What can they do to me? The mountain lion does not eat the dead."

"Will I come with you?"

"No one must know where my body stays. But you will go with me a ways. You must be ready."

"I am making myself into a woman like you said..." Maggie leaned her head on Grandmother's shoulder.

"Good. Now you know." Grandmother let go of her hand. "Drink water," she told Maggie. "Drink and we will go."

They walked back to la ranchería slowly. Maggie kept her arm in Grandmother's most of the way. She did not seem to mind. Maggie knew she must keep what Grandmother had told her to herself. What happens when they ask for you, though? she wanted to ask. But she kept silent. Grandmother would tell her what was necessary. Maggie willed aside what she had heard, but La Madre took on new importance and new meaning. She wanted to hold anger against the mountain. La Madre would take her Grandmother and there was nothing she could do! Then she knew that was not right either. It was a sacred pact between the two of them. This is what Grandmother meant for her to know. And though she could not understand it all, she now saw La Madre with new reverence and love. And so she came to a new place of acceptance with what she knew and began to run a few steps ahead as they walked. Grandmother had been waiting for this but when she saw it a little water ran in the creases of her face. *Los adioses no se dicen como nada,* she said to herself. Goodbyes are not said as if they are nothing. And then her eyes resumed their characteristic distance.

In this way, the skinny long-legged girl running ahead and the old Yaqui woman walking solidly behind carrying the bag of jojoba beans and water jug in one hand while with the other she jabbed at the ground ahead with the point of her stick—in this way and in their own time, they reached home. At peace with what the heart knew would be, they reached home together.

Chapter 10

▲

One morning Maggie woke up to his shouting.

"Where did you hide the money the old lady gave you?"
she heard, and an indistinct answer from her mother.
Maggie got up and crept to the door, opening it when she
heard the crash of furniture. She saw Frank holding a
chair aloft with both hands and Mariana cowering down
by the side of the bed. "Give me the money or I'll kill you,"
he was saying.

"There's no money," her mother cried. "You took it all
already." Frank stopped with the chair still raised above
his head when he saw Maggie wide-eyed in the doorway.

"She doesn't have any money!" Maggie shouted at
him, taking a few steps into the room.

"*No entres.* Do not come in," Mariana pleaded.

"You took it all," Maggie repeated without taking her
eyes off him. In her anger she was not afraid and glared

at him from narrowed eyes. He looked from one to the other, his thickened, once handsome face becoming indecisive and then slick with cunning. He made an attempt to laugh while lowering the chair and coming towards her. She backed up against the door, suddenly feeling naked in her flannel nightgown. Crossing her arms over her blossoming chest, she watched him come closer. She was now as tall as Mariana.

"We're just playing," Frank said, nodding towards Mariana, who was slumped by the bed with one hand over her mouth. Maggie refused to budge.

"Aw, come on," he said, stumbling forward. He caught his balance leaning on the back of the chair, breathing hard. "We're just playing, Chiquita. Come on, I'll show you. I can show you how to make gloves so we can box," he offered.

Maggie looked at Mariana but she made no sign. "What do you mean, you can make gloves?" Maggie was interested in spite of herself.

"Ca'mere," he gestured, going over to the sewing basket. He pulled bunches of socks out and pushed her into the kitchen. He made her put out her hands, wadded up some socks and stuffed them against the palms of her hands, putting more socks over her fists. Then he made some gloves for himself.

"See?" He made a quick jab at her. She dodged and landed an unexpected blow on his arm. She got excited, hitting him twice on the chest. They parried for a few seconds when he suddenly hit her hard on the face. She was pushed backwards a few steps. Determined, she tried to hit him back but he was bobbing up and down like a boxer and laughing. "Come on," he challenged. "You can hit me." She lunged at him, catching him on the chin with a quick left fist. Her laughter was cut off by a hard punch to the head that knocked her down.

"Damn you," she said, struggling to get up.

"What did you say?" He advanced on her.

"Damn you," she repeated, pushing herself up from the floor. He hit her again, knocking her over.

"What did you say?" he repeated.

"You heard me." She was trying to get up.

"What did you say?"

She tried to swing at him but he shoved her hard and she fell against the wall.

"Where did you get that hair from, anyway?" he taunted. "Did anybody ever tell you it doesn't go with those chink eyes?"

"From my *father*. My *real* father," she shouted.

"You have no father!" he laughed. She jumped at him, hitting him on the face. This infuriated him and he instantly punched her back harder.

"Say it. Just say it again," he threatened.

There were tears in her voice now. "Damn..." He hit her again and she fell again. Her head was ringing and the room seemed upside down. She gritted her teeth but she began to cry and couldn't get up.

"I told you," he said. "I told you but you had to keep on talking, didn't you?" He went over and picked up a newspaper, sat down on her bed and started reading it. Still crying, Maggie got up with an effort and threw herself out the door. She stood against the door shivering in her bare feet. Her shame at being beaten was so great she wouldn't go back inside to get anything. She walked slowly past the woodpile and the pomegranate trees. Crying harder, she unlatched the gate and began walking down the dirt road towards the hediondilla.

The sun was just coming up. She saw the beauty of the sky, pink clouds moving and alive. She cried for something she could not have put into words. She yearned to feel from her family an equivalent of how beautiful the world was, how sweet the morning air. The pain of not having this was greater than the pain in her body. She could not name it, but it was love she wanted and longed for. Simply love, and play, and sanity in those near her.

"He hit me! He hit me again," she cried aloud. But her mama would only say, "Well, you know it. If you make him mad, he'll hit you. So why do you open your mouth?" There could be no comfort there or protection. Maggie went without knowing where she was going. Remembering how he had tricked her again into playing with him —games she always lost—only to beat her in the end, she ran hard down the road.

Blood was coming heavily from her nose. She squatted in the dirt holding her head back, swallowing the blood. The inside of her mouth was bleeding too and she spit out a bunch of saliva mixed with blood. Still sobbing, she walked a ways into the chaparral to a big ironwood tree. Crawling underneath its branches she put her arms around the tree. With her face pressed against the gnarled bark, she ceased to cry at last.

The sun rose higher warming the cold earth. The sun's rays reached beneath the ironwood to warm her feet. Comforted by the sparrows emerging from the thickets presenting their bright lives to her eyes and to her heart, she forgot everything. She slept, her fingers curled around the tree. Responding to the voice of the desert, her child's soul knew peace.

"Let her give him the money," Grandmother said to Maggie's complaint.

"But why?"

"Because money itself is not worth anything."

"How would we live?"

"You won't lack, you'll see."

But Maggie didn't see. If this was the new world, then she knew more about it than Grandmother. She knew that money was used to buy things and that they had very little. If it were not for the money Grandmother gave them, what would happen? Grandmother made big cans of posol and menudo on Sundays, the best in the rancherías, and people came after church to buy. With that money they had enough, she said. And after the rainy season started they picked fresh quelites every morning. They grew wild in damp places but had to be eaten before they reached their seeding cycle. They didn't last forever. The women from El Barrio Central went into the monte in the early mornings and picked quelites and then made big pots of quelites con frijoles guisados. They were quick to invite anyone passing to join in eating. On Saturday mornings Maggie went to the grocery store in El Pueblo and waited for Enrique to come to the back door. After he watered and cleaned the produce he gave her a paper bag full of vegetable leaves. Without calling attention to it, he often threw in whole carrots or other vegetables. Enrique was crazy about Grandmother and Maggie accepted the vegetables for her, but every other week she took the bag home to her own house.

Maggie had grown accustomed to her mother's silence. More and more Mariana sat by herself in the rocking chair by the window sewing or not sewing but only picking at the colored threads. If food was put in her hands she ate but she did not seem to know if she was hungry or not. Sometimes Frank showed up and Maggie kept silent seeing the shy happy smile on her mother's face. "Working across the border," he would say and maybe he would bring something, tortillas or coffee or even a piece of meat—the things he liked to eat and which he finished before he left again. Maggie left the house when he was there, staying out in the chaparral or sleeping under the pomegranate trees. In bad weather she kept to her small place in the kitchen.

Without thinking about it, Maggie was often hungry. She tried not to be there when they were eating all the time, but she often visited her nina after school instead of going home. Maggie helped Consuelo until it was time to eat and she was always offered beans and tortillas. She was never sure if Josepha liked her or not—the elder sister was always stern. But her nina always welcomed her with smiles. And she could laugh and chatter with Consuelo who was never upset about anything. Now that she was old enough to go about El Pueblo at will, Maggie found joy in this. When she walked in the door of Las Hermanas she was treated like a grownup.

This day Maggie saw her nina sitting by the sewing machine when she entered the house. She went to see what Consuelo was doing in the kitchen while Emma called, *"Es la Margarita.* It's Margarita," to Josepha's question. The only sister who could read English, it was Josepha's job to deal with household business. She had papers in front of her now.

"How is your mama?" Emma asked the same question every time.

"Lo mismo. The same."

"Take care of her well," Emma always said next. Maggie saw Consuelo through the open door. She was working out by the ramada. Maggie always felt like there was no anger in Consuelo against anybody. Her big round face was always creased in good humor. But today she excused herself soon after Maggie greeted her and went inside. Consuelo had gone to her bed, Emma said, grumbling. "She says she doesn't feel well but laziness is what she has," Emma complained to Josepha.

"Well, if she doesn't feel well, let her lie down," said Josepha. Emma put a bad face on it but when she saw Maggie's concern, smiled at her.

Consuelo had gone to her small place at the side of the house. She sat on the bed for a moment and then tried to get up. It was her intention to return to the kitchen and continue working, but she took a step and fell. She tried to get up but her body would not move. She stayed there. She looked like she was sitting on the floor by the bed intentionally. She had one arm on the bed ready to get up. But she did not move again.

When her nina asked her to stay and eat, Maggie refused. She was hungry but she was sad that Consuelo had not come back and she said goodbye. Instead of going home, Maggie looked over her sack of marbles and decided to go down to the rio. She walked along the rocks for awhile and then went up on the bridge. Bale and Eddie were there with some older boys from El Barrio Central. The younger boys and their little sisters were throwing rocks into the barranca, seeing who could make the biggest splash. She hailed the boys, "Hey you guys, who wants to play marbles?" A couple of them turned around. "For keeps?" Seeing their interested but cautious faces, Maggie said, "The first game for fun and the second for keeps." One of the boys pulled out a sack of marbles and motioned her over to the riverbank. He got a stick and drew a circle on the ground for the ring.

By the time she won the first game, enough kids had gathered around that the loser couldn't refuse the second game. Maggie lost her blue steely on the opening shot. She was so mad she decided to stop being nice and wiped out the kid and all his best marbles.

"You're a girl. You shouldn't be playing marbles anyway," he said disdainfully.

"I can play better than you," she taunted back.

"Yeah, but you're not allowed to play at school. You don't get to play in the tournament." He ran away.

She yelled after him, "That's because I'd slaughter you!" But she knew he was right. It didn't matter how good she was. She couldn't play at school where it counted. Well, at least she wasn't bored anymore, that was for sure. She walked with Bale and Eddie down along the river. They tried to sidestep the puddles of water in their way.

"I wish I was old enough to run away."

"What's old enough?" Bale felt old enough for anything.

"Maybe fifteen. Old enough to get a job."

"What about your Ma?"

"What about yours?" Eddie was dragging his pantlegs in the puddles. Maggie stopped to roll them up.

"Anyway, I'm never running away," said Bale. "I'm staying here forever."

They stood looking around at what he meant. The tamarack trees nearest the rio hung their blossoming branches over the banks. Their pink and white blossoms covered the trees and the ground beneath, the sweet scent filling the air and drawing bees and insects.

"I'm gonna get my own junebug this year," Eddie announced.

"Whadda you mean your own junebug?" scoffed Balestine. "If he's gonna be yours, then you have to tie the thread on him too." Seeing the look on Eddie's face, Maggie nudged him. "Don't worry, Eddie, I'll do it for you." She disliked the way the bugs smelled but tying the thread under the junebug's carapace made it into a great flying machine. And Eddie's triumphant grin was worth her promise. "See? See?" he said to his big brother.

"Aaahh, who cares? You'll get it all tangled up and it'll get away anyway."

Maggie pushed Bale into a puddle. "Stop it! He's only a little kid," she shouted at him.

"I'm gonna get you for that." He ran after her. But Maggie easily outran him. She waved goodbye from the riverbank and went through the jacales of La Milpa up on the slope of Los Quates. She could see everything from there, the houses, the bridge, all of La Milpa. It was spring. Green things flourished along the river amid the soft colors of brown and pink earth. The jacales were white and brown and grey and black. A smokestack rose here and there with smoke drifting serenely into the air. The happy sounds of playing kids blended with the landscape into a harmonious whole. "I'm staying here forever," Bale had said. Maggie sighed, "They *would* stay here forever."

El Cuento:

Pues, iba un Yaqui entre las ramas un día. Iba lejos porque iba a visitar a su familia que vivía en el monte. Y la única cosa que traía para defenderse si pasaba algo era un garrote grande. Pues, de repente le salió una víbora cruzando por el camino y el Yaqui le pegó con el garrote pero no la pudo matar antes de que se metiera en la selva. Pues siguió el Yaqui por el camino. Entonces vio un pueblo y muchos Yaquis arriba del monte onde no había visto nada. Un Yaqui vino y le dijo que el alcalde quería hablar con él. Entonces se presentó enfrente del alcalde y los jefes del pueblo. Le preguntaron que porqué le había pegado a una de las muchachas del pueblo y casi la había matado. Pues, no, dijo el Yaqui, yo no vi a nadie. Pues entró la jovencita y dijo sí, él es el que me pegó, y traía la jovencita unos trapos con yerbas alrededor de su cintura. Pues no, no fui yo, dice éste. Esta vez le vamos a perdonar dice el jefe, pero no le hagas otro daño a nadien que encuentres en el camino. Entonces lo dejaron ir y se fue caminando hasta que llegó con su familia y allí les platicó todo lo que había pasado. Su primo le dijo, pues el pueblo que vistes era el pueblo de las víboras y el jefe era el jefe de todas las víboras. La jovencita fue la víbora que quisistes matar en la selva. Ahora si te encuentras con una víbora cruzando el camino en frente de tí, déjala ir porque no te está haciendo ningún daño.

The Story:

Well there was a Yaqui going through the bushes one day. He was going a long ways because he was going to visit his relatives who lived in the mountains. And the only thing he had with him to defend himself in case something happened was a big club. Well all of a sudden a snake appeared crossing the trail and he struck at it with his club but was not able to kill it before it got into the jungle. The Yaqui continued on down the trail. Then he saw a village and many Yaquis on top of the mountain where he had seen nothing before and a Yaqui came to him and told him the Chief wanted to talk to him. So he presented himself before the Chief and the leaders of the village. They wanted to know why he had beaten one of the young women of the village and almost killed her. Well, no I didn't, said the Yaqui. I didn't see anyone. The young woman entered and said, Yes, he is the one who beat me, and she had some bandages with herbs tied about her chest. Well no, it wasn't me, said the Yaqui. This time we're going to forgive you, said the Chief, but don't ever do harm to someone you meet on the trail. Then they let him go and he continued traveling until he reached his relatives and there he told them all that had happened. His cousin told him, Well the village you saw was a snake village and the Chief was the leader of all the snakes. The young woman was the snake you tried to kill in the jungle. From now on if you meet a snake crossing the trail in front of you, let it go because it is not doing you any harm.

Chapter 11

▲

Bale was lying under a mesquite looking up at the sky, watching the hawks. Red tails burning in the sun, the pair wove patterns around each other. Wheeling and diving, rising and falling back from the zenith at the last possible moment. Brushing stiff black hair away from his eyes he gazed with joyous intensity at the sky. At the hawks leaving trails of crystalline dots in their wake. He saw them with something other than just his eyes; apprehended the patterns they made in their entirety. Gazing with open mouth and dark unblinking eyes, breathing short and quick like the birds. This was like a gift from the heavens to him. They flew only for the beauty of it and for love of each other, belonging to their patch of blue sky like Bale, not thinking, belonged to the desert and the mountains. He let his eyes close, sighing deeply. Opening them again as two gunshots sounded. He saw the hawks hanging in the air next to each other and then one fell heavily off to the side, dead in the air; the other, flapping wildly, careened and went down, one of its legs shot away. With his whole body Bale felt her crash into the ground.

"I *told* you these rattlers 'ud bring us good luck!" Bale ran towards the victory whoops of the two men. Attired in fatigues and cowboy hats, they were squirting beer at each other while holding aloft one of the hawks, head still attached to its body by a tendon. Bale found the other hawk first, heard her gasping, beak splintered where she had bounced off the rocks. Her breast was soaked with blood; one leg stretched and then nothing.

The men had not seen Bale and they came tramping through the underbrush, the one holding up his trophy in one bloody hand and with the other shaking freshly cut rattles.

"Where did you get those?"

The man's eyes narrowed at the appearance of Bale and his accusatory tone of voice.

"Offa dead rattler that'll be one less to bite you, if it's any of your business."

Bale wanted him to understand about the hawks, about the cascabel. "They belong here..." he was pleading.

"Listen kid, I'm not gonna argue with you about rattlers." The man squished the can he was holding with one hand and squirted the last drops of frothing beer all over his mouth. He nodded at the other man, "Bax, get the bird."

"No!" Bale lunged between them, the word coming out half choked from his tightened throat. The other man pushed Bale easily out of the way. "We gone to a lot of trouble gettin' these feathers, kid."

"They're not yours! What gave you the right..."

"*We* gives us the right, thas who!"

Bale grabbed for the hawk that was being shaken in his face and the head came off in his hand. The man got him in a neck grip, the bloody headless bird jammed against his cheek. He was in a vise so tight he could hardly breathe and the smell of feathers and blood made him sick.

"Take it easy, kid. I'm not gonna hurt you." The man laughed as Bale struggled to get free.

"Hey, Jack," the other one said. "Keep holding him. You like these birds so much, maybe you like their fresh blood too." Bale twisted in genuine fear when the blood-soaked neck of the dead hawk was shoved against his face. But then when he tasted the warm blood on his lips and tongue, a tremor went through him the length of his body. He would have cried but held as he was, he could only swallow convulsively.

"Shit, he likes it!" The man holding him shoved him away in disgust and he fell backwards still clutching the hawk's head in one hand. The man was sneering at Bale while retrieving his rifle from the ground. "Yeah, it makes you sick, doesn't it?" said the other one, throwing his beer can in Bale's direction. It landed under a mesquite.

"Bet you can't hit the top of that cactus!" They had forgotten him already. Bale heard them going away, firing shots as they went. He heard the punk! punk! of bullets fired into saguaro flesh. "Fuckin' cactus," from far away.

Bale lay on the ground. Rage and sorrow battled with shame inside of him. He smoothed the feathers on the hawk's head tenderly, his fingers trembling. Like a small boy, he wanted to howl with fury and grief. But the man he thought he should be made him grip his teeth together. And in his anguish, fingers and lips smeared with the blood of the hawk, he wanted to die. He wanted to feel his bones crushed and his life running out in his blood because it was the only way he could imagine to stop the pain he was feeling in his heart.

Bale walked slowly in the direction taken by the two men. Their trail of wasted shells and scuffled sand was easy to follow. He walked along breathing hard, looking under mesquites and along the edges of the sandy wash. Finally, he saw what he was looking for: signs of dry blood on the rocks. Looking more carefully he found the body of the dead cascabel. The ants were already at work scurrying around the cruelly smashed head, the split carcass.

Bale knelt and looked long and curiously at death. He put his fingers inside the broken flesh and ran his hands along the silken scales down to the end where the rattles counting the years of the snake's life had been.

"*Dios en tu cielo.* God in your heaven," he whispered. "Why did You let them know how to reach all the way here? Why, damn you?" he shouted. "Damn you!" He did not know if he was cursing the white men or God.

Chapter 12

▲

That year seemed to take forever. Maggie was lonely no matter where she went. One Sunday she was on her way to visit Grandmother and decided to go through La Milpa. When she reached the bridge, she saw a bunch of boys gathered at the railing. One she didn't know called something to her as she approached. Another pushed him away and she saw that it was Balestine. The boy who had called out laughed and looked away.

Maggie was aware that the Levi's she wore were too tight and too short, that her blouse had a tendency to open when she walked. As she passed, Balestine smiled and said, "Hi." She answered but didn't stop. She walked across the bridge quickly, deciding to walk upriver rather than go past the houses of El Barrio Central.

There was not much water but it was cooler walking along the riverbed among the tamarack. It seemed like she had not seen Bale for a long time. After spending so much of their lives together in other years, it was strange that things had grown awkward between them. It was not that he was so much taller now, but his face was different, silent.

Well, who cared anyway. She dismissed him from her mind and skipped the rest of the way along the stones until she reached the railroad trestle spanning the river. There were no trains so she went along the tracks towards the rancherías. She wanted to pretend that everything was fine as she skipped from log to log and practiced balancing on the rail. But it was not as much fun as when she was little and had played with Bale and Eddie on the tracks. There used to be so many trains passing by. They would sit beside the tracks and count the cars going by from as far away as North Carolina. Sometimes the trains had two or three engines pulling flatbeds loaded with shiny new cars and trucks. Maggie stood holding the long stick she had picked up, gazing up and down the tracks. There was nothing to see but heatwaves dancing above the railroad bed. Crabgrass was growing everywhere, long green blades pushing up from the gravel. She threw the stick down and walked the rest of the way alongside the track, stumbling over the rocks and uneven ground. She was glad to see the white walls of the nearest ranchería. She ran most of the way cutting across the fields of the Quatillos. When she saw one of the Quatillo kids on horseback her heart was lightened and she waved eagerly in greeting. Grandmother was at the sink, cleaning her bellota jars when Maggie arrived, hot and tired at the door.

"*E tu mamá?* And your mama?" Grandmother inquired.

"Fine, fine," Maggie said quickly.

"Did you see if she needed anything?" Grandmother's sharp eyes examined her.

"She didn't say she did," Maggie defended herself. She was angry and hurt. Why did she have to do everything? She sat down and started to cry.

"What's wrong? Don't tell me I'm spanking you?"

"I don't know," Maggie sobbed. "Everything's different," she blurted out. Grandmother said nothing but continued cleaning her jars. Wiping each lid carefully, she placed the jars in the dark coolness of the shelves under the sink. Then she poured two cups of hot water from the kettle steaming on the stove. She searched among her small jars of herbs for the right one, and put a few sticks of something in the cup. After a few moments, she took the sticks out, sniffed the cup and gave it to Maggie who now had hiccups from running so far and then crying.

"Drink it all," Grandmother said. "And now what?"

"Mama doesn't do anything anymore. And I don't have anybody to play with and how come there aren't any more trains?" She began crying anew at this last.

Grandmother sipped her own tea and looked about the room. There was nothing here she would miss if it were taken away, nothing she could not live without, even the stove. Cracks were appearing on the ceiling again. She would have to climb the ladder and patch the walls. Maybe get up on the roof to see what shape it was in for the next winter. And this girl didn't know what to do with herself!

As though she were picking up in the middle of a story, Grandmother said, "Your mama was not taught anything useful, never, only how to embroider and to look pretty. Your father loved a pretty picture." She fixed Maggie with her eyes. "But after the revolution there was no place for pretty pictures."

"I don't care," Maggie said with a low voice.

"Why not? Are you afraid to forgive a little?"

"I'm just a little girl," said Maggie stubbornly. "You say so yourself all the time."

"Yes, I see it," said Grandmother dryly. She shuffled to the door, opened the screen and spit. "And much younger than even I believed." She did not turn but stood in silhouette, looking at the mountains.

Maggie made her voice small. "My mama never took care of me right."

"And so what is that? Mamas live and die like anyone else."

Maggie finished her tea in silence. Her face was tight with tears and her throat scratchy when she said, "But I want to stay here and do things for you..."

"I don't have need of this. Your mama over there needs you more."

Then Maggie knew there was no use in saying more. Grandmother went outside and when Maggie rinsed her cup and looked out, she saw her vigorously hoeing the ground around her lemon tree.

"Are you going now?" Grandmother's voice sounded the same, as though she had not said any of the hard words she had said before. Maggie tried to make her voice the same also, as though it didn't matter. "I'll be back..."

"Good." Grandmother was digging a circle around the tree to hold the water in.

Maggie walked slowly away. She stood for a moment at the edge of the ranchería uncertain of which way to go, and then took the trail leading to the Barrio. She did not even feel like passing through Cien Milla today. It was late anyway, she said to herself, and time to be getting home. She widened her stride and was soon gone around a bend in the trail.

She did not know that Grandmother had come to the back of the house to watch her until she was out of sight. She did not regret the words she had spoken—time was passing and she could not wait forever. And the world that Maggie must live in was coming faster and faster. A shadow passed in front of the sun and she reached out a shaking hand to steady herself against the corner of the house. Bueno, she thought, I will not have to climb the roof too many more times. She chuckled, showing the space between her teeth. Then she went back to making a hole for the new rose cutting she had picked up from someone who had pruned their bushes. To make life out of everything—what else mattered?

Chapter 13

▲

That year the mild days and cold evenings of spring became the long, intensely warm days and short night-times of summer. The first crop of green corn at La Milpa ripened early, but the ears were small and sparsely kerneled. The insects and worms, sensing the weakness of the grain, attacked the crop with vigor. In disgust, the men did not bother to pick the ears but left them to dry in the sun. The second crop ripening in late summer was better, but there were no large eatings of green corn tamales that year. The women of La Milpa made what they made and kept it within their own families. The people from las rancherías bought vegetables from the farmers in Mexico as far south as Cananea and were grateful for the health of their animals.

At the end of every summer Grandmother made jam from prickly pear fruit. Maggie picked the cactus fruit for her as it ripened along the lower slopes of Los Quates. One day she saw Balestine sitting on some rocks overlooking La Milpa. She almost turned to go back the other way but something about the way he looked made her go up to him shyly. She was standing before him when he glanced up. He was happy to see her and she sat down. Together they looked out towards the old cottonwoods shimmering in the afternoon breeze. The fields spread out beneath them. The corn season was over but the stalks still stood tall and green. The beans were left to dry on the plant. Only the melons were still growing, long trailing vines making green patches here and there. A covey of sparrows flew over the slope, veering off to the south. Their bird song came sweetly to the ear until it was suddenly drowned out by a plane flying in low over their heads. The peacefulness of the moment was broken. Bale stood watching the plane.

"There're planes flying over all the time now." His voice sounded too neutral, unemotional.

"It's the SAC command. I heard some of the men talking about it at the shooting range," said Maggie.

He laughed. "What were you doing there? Oh yeah, I remember, the hole near the center is your bullet!"

Maggie laughed too. "That was a long time ago."

"You're still shooting? I think that's great." He seemed to really mean it. She was pleased. When he laughed, he was the friend she remembered. The one with the ready grin on his face, his hair hanging in front of his eyes. Now it smelled like hair oil. She felt shy again. But he didn't notice. "So how do you like high school?" He picked up a rock and threw it.

"Okay. And you?"

He shrugged. He put his hands in his pockets and took them out again. "Maggie, did you know they're not going to grow anything at La Milpa next year? I mean we can still plant what we want around the houses, but they're not going to do the big communal planting anymore."

"But why?" Maggie was stunned. La Milpa had been producing as long as she could remember. Since before Grandmother came here even.

"The men don't think it's worth it anymore. Anyway, since Korea there's hardly enough people to do the work." He threw another rock, hard, over the edge. "I gotta get going," he said over his shoulder, walking away.

"Maybe I'll see you at school," she called after him. He waved in response and was gone.

Maggie finished picking prickly pear fruit absentmindedly. She drew blood from a thorn piercing her fingers more than once. On her way to Grandmother's she thought about things.

Of the three rancherías to the north, only Mariana's was still run in the old way. They had running water, but it came from a well. There was no gas or electricity. They cooked on a wood stove, grew a few vegetables and raised some chickens and rabbits for eggs and meat. They had a small plot of green corn and a few beans—the things that grew largely by themselves. She had to admit to herself it was getting harder to keep things going. Most of the time when she looked up Mariana would just be standing there holding the hoe and looking at nothing. They no longer depended on what they grew, and they were the only ones doing that much. The Carrillo place had been empty for a long time, and the Ochoas hardly came outside since the youngest boy had been shot in Korea. At first the house had been full with those going over to see him and hear the story of how he was machine-gunned. But he was always in the VA now and people had stopped going around. One time she had seen the old man and woman walking down the road carrying bags of groceries. They had barely spoken as they passed. She knew the other boy had moved into town. He had a new car and a girlfriend and Maggie never saw him passing on the road now.

On the other side of El Pueblo lived Las Hermanas in their ranchería, but they didn't grow anything. They were too old. They harvested quelites and went each year to the gathering of bellota like everyone. But they lived mainly from her nina's pomadas. Her mother had been a well-known curandera and had passed her secret recipes for healing salves to Emma. She treated people from the Barrio for things like boils, wounds and various pains.

In Las Rancherías Chiquitas there was Grandmother, the Quatillos who still planted alfalfa, and the Stones. They were gringos but they had been around as long as Grandmother and spoke Spanish as well as the natives. Old man Stone didn't work anymore, and the girls had married and gone. Not one of them had wanted to stay. They said they wanted something better for their kids. Mrs. Stone had been over to Grandmother's one day telling the whole story and wiping her eyes.

"How come she was telling you?" Maggie had asked after the woman left. "You don't even say anything back."

"Mrs. Stone cares much for me. When you were little, she was the one who brought us food many times."

Maggie was surprised. "How come?"

"Los años...." was all Grandmother would say. Maggie remembered hearing that when the Stone boy was killed on the tracks, it was Grandmother who went with Mrs. Stone to get the body and to fix it and she stayed with Mrs. Stone until the rest of the family came back from wherever they were. Maggie guessed it was things happening and people handling it together that made them close.

Grandmother had a few chickens and was always talking about getting rid of those. She didn't keep rabbits anymore. One day she had seen one of hers pop its head out of the ground in Cien Milla! She had come home and plugged up their holes in the pen and left them to their own devices. What else? Grandmother still used lanterns, but she didn't believe in burning much light after dark anyway. She got water from her well, heated it on the stove and took a bath in front of the fire in a bandeja like they all did. Well, what was great about that? It's not about hot water and electric lights, she answered her own question. That's not what makes Bale feel bad and me crazy. It's...I don't know. But something is happening. We used to look out and see the desert, and now there is nothing. We used to see the land and the mountains and now everywhere we look there are houses of the gringos. We exist in patches that they don't see. Another way of doing things is right in our faces and we haven't even realized it. The worst part is they don't even know we're here.

"Oh you think you figured it all out, huh?" said Bale when she told him about it. They were eating sandwiches at school. There were a few kids from La Milpa and another few from El Barrio Central. Maggie was the only one from a ranchería. They could have been from another planet to the white kids from the project houses. So they sat eating their bologna sandwiches because they didn't want anybody to see them eating tortillas, not even each other. None of them had money for the cafeteria so they hung around outside, sitting on the tables, their feet on the benches, like it didn't matter.

"Why? Am I wrong?" asked Maggie.

"You're not wrong. There's just more to it, mucho más. They not only don't know we're here, they don't care that we've been here for a long long time. This was our land."

"Hey, it belongs to the guy that can buy it!" said another boy. "And we sure as hell can't."

"It doesn't just have to do with some money," said Bale. "Our world has become invisible."

"Yaaaa, we're invisible! The invisible man!"

"Go ahead and laugh. You'll find out when los americanos are right next door and they tell you you can't have chickens or goats anymore."

"Who wants to be stepping on chicken mierda all your life?" The boy jumped down from the table, sailing his smashed-up lunch bag through the air at the trash can.

"You missed," someone said.

"It's *their* school, let *them* clean it up!" he said and sauntered away.

"He's stupid," Maggie said.

Bale shrugged. "Who cares anyway?"

But Maggie couldn't stop thinking about it.

Chapter 14

▲

Those years were years of contradictions for Maggie. Her mind was filled with inconclusive images of the world, her body with intimations of change. Her heart sang and suffered in shifting balance between youth and old age. She grew dark brown from the sun. Walking the old desert trails became too familiar for her. She grew too wise for the innocent voices of the doves in Cien Milla, and at times too angry. Her hunger to understand the world was still there. But she saw things. The world she thought was a mystery came close with the easily comprehensible: rock 'n roll, department stores, national park designations. She enjoyed access to places and things typical in the life of a teenager in a rapidly growing town in America, USA. She trooped with the rest of her classmates to the five 'n dime to listen to 45s, practicing the new dance steps in the restroom during recess. She put on and rubbed off bright red lipstick, whispered about padded bras.

And the world she thought she knew everything about became the mystery. As it always had been without her knowing. She had yet to know her real identity, her true self. But she was getting ready to reach out and touch it.

En El Día

Ya ves hija, hay veces que buscamos nuestro camino sin saber y sin querer. Por eso tenemos que estar listas. Que tenga o que no tenga nombre, el poder lo tenemos adentro.

During the Day

You see, daughter, there are times when we seek our path without knowing or wanting to. That is why we must be ready. Power is inside of us whether it has a name or not.

Chapter 15

▲

It was spring and the wild crops flourished as before: mesquite beans, prickly pear fruit and bellota—the acorns swelling and ripening with the monsoon rains of August. Maggie and Grandmother traveled to the southern mountains, living out in the open with Las Hermanas and other people from La Milpa. Here they gathered acorns, filling sack after sack for the winter months ahead. The men climbed to the topmost branches of the ancient gnarled trees while the women spread blankets on the ground below. The men shook the branches and the acorns fell in showers, to the squeaking delight of the children.

When the rains and lightning fell, the women prayed beneath their canvas shelters, cradling the infants. The older children proved they were older by ignoring warnings and racing around under the pelting rain. But when the lightning came near they ran for shelter to their fathers, much to the amused smiles of all. Sometimes the lightning came so close, it charged by the tents with a dreadful sssssss. Seconds later, a deafening roll of thunder burst in their ears. The children jumped and laughed to ease their fear. But the violence of the storms came and went quickly. Half dollar raindrops became mist and the winds blew holes in the billowing grey clouds and spread open the sky above the hills. The rays of the afternoon sun gave the people faith in the constancy of the heavens.

On warm sunny mornings, Maggie spread their cache of acorns to dry before cleaning away the leaves and twigs. She also helped her nina, who no longer could see very well, to remove any rotten acorns and then pack them for the trip back. Like the others she always carried a pocketful, eating while she worked. She was adept at cracking an acorn in circular fashion around its center with her teeth, separating the two halves with her tongue and spitting out the shells. To those unacculturated to the flavor, bellota may have tasted too bitter, inedible. But the youngest child there could put away a pound in a single eating and leave a mound of shells behind.

Some afternoons Maggie roamed the nearby hills searching for dried pieces of wood from the winter before. They would be glad for the thick pieces of ironwood when cold weather came again. Mesquite was best for cooking, burning long and evenly and flavoring the food. But ironwood burned hot and long and they depended on it for heat. She cut the pieces into proper size with an axe and piled them in the space reserved for their use in the open-backed communal truck. Since she was always busy, the time passed quickly, and then it was the last night.

That night the men made a big fire and everyone gathered to laugh and tell stories. The stories were often about amusing things that had happened to family members. They were about supernatural events, or stories of disobedient children and what happened to punish them and make them change their ways.

Grandmother sat through the evening quietly. When she was asked, she said, *"Yo? Pa' qué?* Me? What for? Maggie has a story. Tell it," and nudged Maggie.

"Sí, es muy inteligente. Yes, she's very intelligent," Emma said in a proud voice.

But Elmira Balestine butted in, saying, *"Bueno, para qué les sirve la escuela a las mujeres?* Well, what good is school for women? They don't teach them anything about work of the home."

"Since when did you go to school?" said Emma's acid tongue. She would have gone on but Grandmother nudged Maggie hard with her elbow again and Maggie said, "Okay...I have a story."

One time there was a beautiful young woman who was the most beautiful in all El Pueblo. She went everywhere and did everything, but the thing she loved most of all was to dance. She went to all the bailes and of course she had no end of partners and so would dance the night away. She would dance all night and not come home until the early hours of the morning. Well, her padres naturally were upset with this and told her not to go. But she wouldn't listen to them. Even though they told her not to go, she wouldn't obey them.

One night she was particularly beautiful, dancing with every man who asked her, winning all their hearts. And then a man asked her to dance whom she had never seen before. He was so handsome, this young man with beautiful deep eyes, that she wanted to dance only with him. The time came and went when her padres told her to come home and she went on dancing. And then she happened

to look down at his feet and she saw they were the hooves
of a goat. It was el Diablo, the devil himself.

At this point all the listeners were nodding their heads
and making noises affirming the beautiful young woman's
well-deserved end. But one young child said, "So what
happened to her?"

"Well," said Maggie, "she started to faint and go crazy
but then she remembered who she was. She changed into
a black jaguar and bit his head off!"

The kids went "Yeahhhh!" but their padres were silent,
the women trying to gauge the feelings of the men and at
the same time signaling their daughters not to say anything. The same little child said, "So who scared everybody more, the devil or the jaguar?"

"Nobody could see the devil but her, but everybody
saw the black jaguar. So you see there was a lot of running
that night!"

"You see?" said Josepha to Emma later. "That's what
she gets for being with Adela all the time who is nothing
but a savage. And for not going to the Catholic school!"

Emma was torn between agreeing with her sister and
affection for Maggie—after all she was Maggie's nina—so
she made the sign of the cross and resolved to speak
seriously with Maggie about praying to La Virgencita for
guidance and pure thoughts.

Grandmother had been very silent all evening, so in
silence Maggie helped her to get ready for bed: combing
her hair, rubbing her shoulders, bringing her a cup of
water. Then Maggie caught her eye and smiled.

"From where did you get that story?" said Grandmother.

"I thought you told it to me."

"Umph, I've never heard it told like that." She covered her face with her tapalo and rolled herself in her serape to go to sleep. "Just be careful," she muttered from beneath her tapalo, "the devil has many friends."

Maggie lay gazing up at the moon, studying her face and listening to the sounds of crickets. A sense of well-being and peacefulness overcame her. This more southern range of mountains was moister, greener than the mountains of the desert lowlands she was used to. These mountains calmed her heart and made her strong. The gentleness and strength of a black jaguar in repose, she thought. That night, for the first time in her life, she slept with the abandonment of a free spirit.

Chapter 16

▲

"Somewhere over the mountain, 'cross the sea, my true love's waiting for-or me..." The rock 'n roll station Doreen had been listening to was still on, and Balestine sang to himself and to the wide open desert. The car seemed to be moving into space without moving at all, distant mountains receding forever. He looked down at his hands, brown fingers with the tattoo of a cross between thumb and forefinger. The mountains reached in and wrapped themselves around his thoughts.

The car kept going, bouncing on the rough dirt road and always going higher and higher. Finally it stopped in a cloud of dust. Bale got out leaving the car in the middle of the road and sat on the hood. The sun shone down on him and on the old Spanish town. Surrounded by mountains and dotted with cacti, green palms and tamarack, it spread out in all directions. Bale sat looking out over the desert that was home to his ancestors.

The original Balestine had been a muleteer for the Padres. He had even had the courage to climb the Mission scaffold after two others had fallen. His legs quaking and his mouth dry, he had directed the Indios in slapping the last of the whitewash on the adobe walls—for the love of God and for ten years dispensation of his sins. He had also been given two mules which he later lost, along with his own life, in a fall from Colt's Pass. He left three children: one of them was Bale's great-great-grandfather. He took a wife, a Tarahumara who served the Padres by sweeping the dirt floors of the Mission. Every day she swept while repeating the prayers the Padres taught her, mixing up Spanish words with her own meanings and falling asleep in the flickering lights of the candles.

The Spanish blood of Balestine descendants was never pure again. It was always mixed with the blood of mountain tribesmen, the Tarahumara, the Maya and other Cahitans. Successive generations would alternate between the light-skinned, round-eyed and long-lashed Españoles and the dark-skinned, slanted-eyed and squat-bodied Indios.

The Padres moved south. After years of hardship, some returned to Spain. Others remained and lay buried in the small graveyard behind the Mission. And at least one member of the Balestine family continued to serve them.

The women sewed pretty white cassocks worn underneath by the priests and also by the statues of saints. They tended the flowers that decorated the altar on feast days. The men swept the clay floors and wore out the stone with their kneeling. But after Bale's father died he felt like that was the end of it. In his quiet way, without protesting, he came to believe less and less. He went to confession on Easter and Christmas only to make his mother happy but he did not care what the Church said. It wasn't true the good were rewarded. His father and mother had never done anything but live for the Church. But his father was dead a long time ago and the family lived in poverty along the banks of the Rio. His mother still went often to the Mission and kissed the Archbishop's ring. Once when Bale was a little boy, the Archbishop had walked unexpectedly into the courtyard and Bale's mother had whispered quickly that he should do as she did. She kneeled and kissed the extended hand. Not knowing it was the ring she kissed, Bale had kissed the Archbishop's finger. He still remembered the feel of the Archbishop's hairy knuckle on his lips. Confused and embarrassed at the same time without knowing why, he had backed away behind his mother's skirt. Now he knew those feelings were the beginning of the absurdity he would always feel towards the practices of the Church; not just what they did, but also the meaning behind it. The Archbishop had continued to lift his hand and murmur the sign of the cross in blessing. And then he had hurried away in his black dress, the one he wore around his house. In answer to his question, Bale's mother told him the priests' house was the Church. But he saw the Archbishop go into a building, and he wondered what was behind the door where the Archbishop went? There was never any way to peek inside. Las Hermanitas always kept them at the door when his mother brought the white things she sewed and ironed. Sometimes las Hermanitas let them stand in the entranceway of the house where they lived. He was mystified by the shadows, the silence and the candles burning in red cups. Sometimes las Hermanitas had bread left from the stuff they made the hosts from. He liked eating the paper-thin circles, although they stuck to the roof of his mouth. He didn't understand why it was okay to chew it then, but they couldn't chew the hosts the priests put in their mouths in church. His mother explained la Hostia wasn't Jesus' body until the priest made it so. He understood he would hurt Jesus if he chewed His body. In his innocence he believed that if he took care of Jesus then nothing would ever happen to his father—Jesus would take care of him the same way. But something had gone wrong. He knew now that one cannot make agreements with God, but the feelings he had experienced when his father had died in a cruel accident could never be erased.

Even now, sometimes alone, he would go into the Mission searching for signs of his ancestors. He walked around, when no one else was there, looking at the strangely wrought expressions of the Santos with their faces always looking up. He imagined the fingers of his ancestors wearing away the paint with their devotions— he felt for them with his own fingers. He saw their lips kissing the feet of Jesus, but whatever the essence of those relationships he could not feel them now. He was alone as he had always been alone. Those to whom he was linked by blood and action were gone forever; nothing could bring them back. Then Bale would run from the cold shadows into the warm sun; he would get as far away as he could from the cold and empty walls.

His ancestors were gone, and now his people were disappearing too. Eddie said it wasn't true, but he knew the desert was shrinking day by day. And the life of the desert was linked to the lives of the people, to his own life. There were more white kids around every day—they had to live some place. Where they lived was in nice new houses with green grass drinking all the water. In those houses they had their own rooms; when they sat down to eat they ate steak and drank big glasses of cow's milk that made them tall and heavy, while he and his brother were thin on beans and tortillas.

"*Andale, come, m'hijo.* Come, my son, eat," his mother begged. "Eat, so you can grow," spooning out the beans. What for? he thought. Look at Eddie—he was a year and a half younger but he was taller than Bale. He had the Spanish blood. It showed in his handsome open features and light skin. Bale had wide shoulders and a large chest, but his legs were short and thin. His eyes were slanted and his straight black hair fell over his eyes.

He didn't know that his chest was bred for breathing the oxygen-thin air of the altiplano not these desert winds. That his eyes were narrowed for peering into long distances in search of danger. If he had lived in the high mountains, he would have had muscle and power in his legs. He sat on the hood of the Ford looking out over the desert. He did not have a contract with God, or the world or even with his own soul. He could find no meaning in his existence. He yearned for another world and the girl in the song...."Over the mountain, 'cross the sea, my true love wa-aits for-or me."

Chapter 17

▲

Balestine and Maggie walked across the field in front of school, watching the shotputters practicing in the late afternoon sun. It was cold and Maggie pulled her jacket closer. Her skirt was too tight; she hiked it up around her knees to climb the bleachers.

"Why don't you get skirts like Doreen?" Bale said, watching her struggle.

"When they give them away at the department store I'll be first in line," Maggie said with a crooked smile.

"Sorry, quedita. I forget when I'm with her."

"It's okay, I hate dresses anyway. I can't wait to get home and put on my Levi's."

"I'm sick of being poor," he said. Maggie stretched her legs out. "Ay!" She was weary of the whole thing. Bale changed the subject. "Do you know what Eddie said this morning? He said he wasn't going out with girls, that he didn't need to do that. He's going to fight the Brahmas."

"He doesn't need girls so he's going to fight the Brahmas to prove he has balls anyway?"

Bale said what he was really thinking about: "Doreen's mother won't let her go out with me." He was staring straight ahead. Maggie had wondered why she always saw them in the car making out before class with Eddie in the front seat keeping track of time.

"I love her," he said.

"So wait until she's eighteen and run off!"

"She won't do it. She wants a big wedding with everybody there." He sat in silent misery.

"She doesn't love you enough. Not like a mexicana."

"I don't want a mexicana. All they think about is getting some gringo to marry them."

"You think every girl is hot to pull down her pants?"

"Take it easy." He tried to reach over and ruffle her hair.

"You want me to understand about Doreen but you don't want to understand what I'm saying, right?"

"Come on, don't get mad," he tried to kid her.

"I have to get mad or I'll go crazy. Nobody knows the reality, the cliques, how the rich kids stick together."

"You seem to get along with them okay."

"Yeah, in class, where they can get the right answer from me or sit next to me to sing on the right note, but when I pass them in the hall they pretend not to see me. No rich gringo kid is gonna look at one of us."

"Why don't you hang out with the chavalas?"

"And talk about lipstick and boyfriends? They don't trust me anyway. Every time they see me coming I feel like I'm waving the enemy's flag in their face with my hair."

"Maybe you don't give them a chance." It was Maggie's turn to sit in silence. Maybe so, but he wouldn't understand why she wanted to talk about books and ideas, not boys. Balestine said, "I'm enlisting in the Army."

"When?" She couldn't believe it.

"I'll be eighteen in two months. They'll let me graduate....My mother wants me to finish high school."

"She's letting you do it?" Her heart hurt.

"She doesn't want me to. She said she'd never sign for me, so I haven't said anything."

"Are you doing this because of Doreen?"

He shifted uncomfortably. "I don't know. No, I don't think so. It's not the main reason. I just don't want to stand around waiting for nothing."

"Listen, I found out you can get a loan for college."

"You have to take stuff in summer school to get in, don't you? I have to work in the garage all summer."

"Can't you work after school and on weekends?"

"I can't do it. Look, it's too late. And I'm not smart enough anyway."

"How do you know? They never told us to take anything but General Ed. Nobody told me I had to be in College Prep to get into college. I just found it out myself."

"Why should they tell us anything? They know we're not going anywhere." She could hear the pain in his voice. And she saw something that scared her: she saw how different he was from this new world of white skins and perfect speaking. She saw how dark he was, how slanted his eyes. And she saw that he saw it too. It scared her and made her want to cry. She put her arm around his shoulder and, doing this, she noticed how clean his clothes were, how creased his pants and polished his shoes. How hard it must be for his mother to keep him and Eddie looking that way. She touched the crease on his pantleg. She started to cry.

"Hey, you're getting me all dirty," he laughed.

"I feel like you're going away forever."

"Bullshit. Anyway, what do you care?" She covered her face with her jacket. "Look, I'll be around," he said more gently. He was confused. Doreen hadn't cried when he'd told her this morning.

They sat side by side on the bleachers. This was where parents would sit on graduation night. He looked up at the mountains. The sky was blue and the mountains were blue but they were so different from each other. It felt funny to say it to himself, but he loved the mountains. He looked down at his shoes, spit-polished to perfection. He spent Saturday afternoons on them. He painted them with a special polish of soap aged in the sun for three days. After that came a layer of wax, put on little by little with his fingers. Then carefully, rolling up both ends of a length of soft cloth, he buffed and slapped at the leather until it shone like a mirror. He looked down now and could see his own face in it. Suddenly he saw the eyes of a hawk, and he couldn't stand it anymore. He just couldn't stand it.

Chapter 18

▲

What does it mean to be poor? Not to have things, but so what? thought Maggie as she walked through a grove of young sage. Under her feet the earth gave way to rutted track where the rain had worn through, a water winding. Or just a track created by insects or an ancient path made long ago by nocturnal animals.

Her feet stepped solidly on the ground, avoiding weak spots and whenever possible the straightforward green things sprouting. The wildflowers had rough skins and a variety of colors but only two or three petals, nothing complex. It was simplicity that survived here. Poor is only poor when someone has more, Maggie went on thinking. But then where does it stop? But the damn gringos have so much, she argued with herself. We start thinking it's our fault because we don't. We start being ashamed at not having what they have, of not being like them. It's like

riding a horse that's racing around without stopping—
how do we get off? It's too late not to get on. Kill the horse?
Maggie suddenly didn't want to explain anything. She
didn't want to see as far as the mountains. She dropped
deliberately through a natural barricade of mesquite,
sliding on the loose dirt and plunging down into the sandy
bottom of a wash.

The wash she broke into was a wide one, maybe twenty
feet across. It continued in the distance ahead until
tamarack trees broke its edge in a curve. Being surrounded by walls of dense growth made her solitude
intense. It made awareness reach beyond her own person,
as though her eyes were a part of everything she saw.
Things kept coming up inside of her too. Everybody else
talked and laughed but Bale just looked at her out of the
depths of himself. She knew sometimes she looked at him
the same way. As if they only really knew each other. He
said he was going into the Army. Why? Their friendship
had limits. Why? Because they looked at each other
across a great distance and that distance was the white
world between them, the world she was forcing herself
into and the world he couldn't fit into. Oh, stop being
melodramatic, she thought. Just talk like them, eat like
them, act like them...what's the big deal? Anybody can
do it. And then one day when we're tired of hiding, we take
off our costume...and what? Who did we fool but each
other? We hurt each other hiding ourselves. That's what
it was with Bale: they were too much alike in hiding what
hurt and they could see it on each other's faces like red
paint. They looked at each other and could do nothing,
only look away. They didn't want to comfort each other;
they only wanted to forget. But sometimes they saw and
remembered.

She kicked at the rocks. It was good to hear the sand
crunch underfoot, to feel her toes curling around the

rocks in her path. It felt good to push against the earth and to be alone with the desert. Right now there was no other world but this one. She knew there were big cities somewhere with many people. But here there was nothing else. There was only her heart beating inside a larger heart. She followed the wash in the direction of the foothills. Looking away from the sun in the western sky she saw hawks wheeling and looping and sweeping past each other with the freedom of wings. The wash abruptly flattened out and she left it, cutting to her left, adjusting slightly to her right, as Grandmother did, preferring to keep La Muerte at her rear. Now that she knew she would keep walking, she began keeping track of inner time. She was judging how long she could go and how long it would take to return. She would know when she got there. She didn't have to think about it; it was something she had learned walking alone in the desert.

Very gently she was going uphill. Without being able to see anything yet—the sage bushes were too thick and tall. She was leaning in her walking and constantly avoiding the small spiny cholla that were everywhere. Decaying cactus nourished the living. Green life sprouted from blackened dried-out skin and woody skeleton. Tiny fuzzy leaves of ground cover were underfoot too and an occasional jojoba plant with its thick rounded leaves and stout bough. This was a place for datura too; she recognized it several times but did not stop. With datura it was better not to say hello if one did not want an extended conversation. The plant was jealous in that way. There was a shift in the wind. She smelled moisture and adjusted her direction more definitively towards the southeast. The ground rose more steeply and the sage became sparser. She could see the foothills and the higher rockier mountain beyond. Rows of clouds were forming horizontally behind the foothills; they would begin to move later. From the smell in the air, wind currents were still moving in the direction she was leaving.

The ground had become harder and steeper, but she moved smoothly and gained the first set of foothills. Looking to the southwest she could already see the low pointed peaks identifying home. They were just distinguishable in the afternoon haze. She looked up at the rocky face of La Madre. The bare sides of her rising upward, the white rock rising out of the reddish earth made her feel how close she was to the mountain, how it had begun to lean on her, how they had begun to participate together to create the totality of this event. It was a common thing to feel, not out of the ordinary. She was beginning to walk in a place where few people had been and the earth was sensitive to her. She placed each foot carefully, barely touching the ground. She breathed slowly and steadily, disturbing nothing with her body or with her presence. Then she was moving down easily and came to a ravine green with scrub. The water there was clean because recent rains had swollen the falls above. She heard sounds—the falls speaking to the mountain. She heard a coyote bark too. One had just been at the water and so she knew of the progression of the afternoon.

It was hot although the season was cool. A wet bandana tied about her neck felt good and refreshing. She rested and sucked one of the two oranges she carried. She kept her own rules of desert movement: it was better to return with supplies than to risk depletion. She rinsed with the cold water from the stream. A trace of minerals clung to the roof of her mouth. She drank to a level of comfort but not to saturation, always training her body. She drank with pleasure. She wet down the canteen to keep the water cool and hung it on her belt. While she was doing this, some swallows arrived, drinking and chirping.

She waited for them to finish so as not to frighten them and then went upstream. She climbed to the top of the ravine and onto the mountain. She was high enough to see the desert now. White lines cut across it, sometimes intersecting or vanishing on the broad expanse. The rocky face of La Madre was now to her right directly above her. As she walked along the high rimside taking easy, almost flat steps, the clouds came lower and closer. And then she stepped upon another kind of ground.

She looked about curiously. The ground was unnaturally flat, but without a sign that it was manmade. It slanted slightly to the southeast and made a kind of rectangle with rounded edges. She walked from one side to the other, circumventing the entire surface. She saw the Santa Teresas running down to a sharp edge in the north. To the west lay Los Quates with its rambling peaks. In the far distant southeast were the mountains facing Las Tinajas near the Mexican border. And the face of La Madre towered above her.

Pale clouds were moving out from behind the face of the mountain and closing out the sunlight above her head. She reached out and put her hands into them. The clouds were like a single entity, soft and dense, warm and cold and cold and warm. Its outer skin was translucent but held all available color inside; aspects of green reflected from the hillside were revealed and then subtly hidden. Her heart beat faster and the windcloud became a silent rushing storm going through her, and then it was as if a path cleared. She saw snakes of life coming towards her out of the mountain and an answering tangle of strands coming out of her own heart. In their meeting she *knew*...that she was the daughter of the mountain. And like the mountain she knew every cactus and rock and tiny lizard. She knew every stick and thorn intimately, felt their common flesh and their common thirst. She under-

stood the singularity of every living thing. Now her aloneness beat against the walls of her heart trying to get out.
But her essence could not be broken.

The first wisps of rain fell upon her face. She was
clenching a stone between her fingers. She only had time
to see it before the rain increased to a smashing downpour. She pressed against the rock wall of the mountain
and watched while waves of rain beat across the sacred
place. The strength of the storm tested all her senses until
the curtain lifted little by little and exposed a beautiful
brown earth dotted with green cacti. A line of blue bleach-
ing to white already lay along the far horizon. The sun was
lower in the west. Too low! She must leave quickly.

She was below the horizon line walking in a bowl-like
expanse of desert. She couldn't see the reddening sky to
the west or take advantage of its light. But mesquite
reflected orange light from the setting sun as it ricocheted
across the desert floor. She drank from the last orange
without slackening her speed, reaching deep for every
drop of energy. She moved with a consistent rhythm. She
could see where things were by the light emitted from
various colors, the greys and yellow-greens. The moon
would not be rising early; it was too soon in her cycle.
Maggie checked her location. She had shortened the
margin by fifteen minutes. But a mile in the desert on a
dark night was a long time. She had walked many times
in the desert alone or with friends. But this night the
darkness was a solid pressure around her and fear was
pushing with a cold hand at her shoulder blades. From
all that had happened, she was too open, too exposed.
She had to close herself up. Her thoughts wandered and
she broke her concentration. She was unsure of her
movements. The rattlers she had seen that morning came
to mind. She had been thinking about Bale, her eyes

dragging momentarily on the ground, and she came around a curve in the trail and the snakes were directly in front of her. They were mating, entwined about each other in a huge rolling loop. She had barely avoided them and now she was all the more frightened knowing how high their venom ran in spring. But snakes were just one small thing in a vast desert and she had never felt this way before. She was afraid. At last she felt the gradual sloping of the ground. She knew she was approaching the edge of the bajada and the road somewhere beyond.

There was a pain in every stride from hard and shallow breathing. And then she heard the sobbing howl of an animal in the darkness directly behind her, the one that had been there all this time, and fear coursed through her. On the brink of surrendering to panic she thrust herself into a stumbling run and suddenly broke out on the rim in visual sight of her markers: two tall saguaros surrounded by barrel cactus. The car would be a few hundred yards to the west in a gully at the bottom of a winding road.

For the first time she was glad for a manmade dirt road and the smells of oil and metal. Unlocking the door to the Buick, she heard the same sobbing howl again. It would not cross the rim. Still shaking she locked herself in and started the engine. She wanted to drown out any other sound. The dark and her aloneness were too great. These feelings were new to her. It was not like it had been on the mountain but it was because of what had happened there that she felt this way. When her heart had opened to love it had opened to fear and confusion too. She could take nothing for granted. La Madre had two faces and one was forever in darkness. She had been given a sacred place for the rest of her life, but already Maggie wanted to be free of it. She wanted to pull away but it came out of the darkness and held her even while she was driving away.

El Cuento:

Me acuerdo que vino un señor y me pidió ayuda para ir a encontrar un tesoro. Me contó que él y otro habían encontrado una cueva en el monte. Entraron y van viendo un tesoro de puras onzas de oro. Entonces se les apareció un espíritu y les dijo: "Pueden llevar todo el oro que quieran pero solamente lo que puedan llevar sobre ustedes mismos." Pues se llenaron las bolsas y los sombreros; hasta se quitaron las camisolas y las amarraron llenas de oro. Entonces el espíritu se hizo esqueleto. Uno de ellos cayó con fiebre y se murió después. Después de muchos años su hijo vino y fue el que me habló. Resultó que les había dicho ése que cuando necesitaran más oro que podían venir a un cierto lugar onde había cuatro caminos y que lo esperaran allí. A las puras doce de la noche cuando la luna estuviera llena iba a venir.

"Pues," le dije al señor, "cómo no, yo voy con usted." Entonces nos pusimos a esperar. Y a las puras doce oímos que venía un caballo, venía y no llegaba. Y otra vez, tras! tras! se oía el ruido de cascos queriendo llegar pero no llegaba. Al fin le pregunté al señor, "Tiene usted una medalla o algo bendito?" "Bueno, sí lo tengo," me dijo y sacó una medalla del Santo Niño que traía cerca de él. "Es por éso que no puede llegar el espíritu," le dije. Así dicen los de la iglesia, que no llega un espíritu donde hay cosa bendita si es un alma perdida.

The Story

I remember that a man came and asked me for help in finding a treasure. He told me he and another man had found a cave in the mountains. They went in and saw a treasure of pure ounces of gold. Then a spirit appeared to them and said, "You can take all the gold you want but only what you can carry on you." Well, they filled their pockets and their hats; they even took off their shirts and tied them full of gold. Then the spirit turned into a skeleton. One of the men fell ill with fever and he died later. After many years his son came and he was the one who spoke to me. It turned out that the spirit had told them when they needed more gold they could come to a certain place where four roads met and wait for him there. At exactly twelve o'clock when the moon was full he would come.

"Well," I said to the man, "sure, of course I'll go with you." So we set ourselves down to wait. And at exactly twelve o'clock we heard a horse approaching; it was coming near but it didn't arrive. And again, pound! pound! we could hear the hoofbeats trying to arrive but they couldn't reach there. Finally I said to the man, "Do you have on yourself a medal or something blessed?" "Well, I do," he said, and took out a medal of the Blessed Child which he carried next to him. "That is the reason the spirit can't arrive," I told him. That's what the ones from the church say: that lost souls cannot come where there is something blessed.

Chapter 19

▲

The day was ending and Elmira Balestine did not have supper ready for her sons. Eddie was all right; he wouldn't come home until his last newspaper was sold. But the other one—how he needed his father. She wiped her eyes with a pañuelo, replacing it in the pocket of her black cotton dress, and continued kneading the dough. As long as there was a bit of flour and some beans they would go on living. It was getting dark but she would not light the lamp so as not to waste oil. She went once more to the window and peered out across the wide banks of the dry riverbed to try to see if the car was coming. Seeing nothing, she put back the curtain and returned to her bandeja. *"Ay Dios mío,"* she quickly made the sign of the cross; let nothing happen to the boys, she prayed.

She squeezed out the balls of masa, arranging them in a circle inside the bandeja. Then she covered everything with a white cloth and went to see to the fire. She put another stick in and wiped the top of the stove. She tested the hotness with a wet finger—it was hot enough. In fact, she had better be quick or the tortillas would cook too fast and be hard to turn. She began pressing out the balls of dough with a tall glass. She spread a couple of tortillas on the stove, letting them puff up, and turned them, using a cloth to press out the steam. As the tortillas cooked, she wrapped them so they would stay hot. Here comes the car, she said to herself excitedly. She stirred the beans and chili in a hurry and put down a plate and cup.

"You've come, my son? Thank God nothing has happened to you," she greeted him.

"What would happen to me, Ma?" He kissed her on the cheek. "Eddie home?"

"Not yet. Sit down so you can eat."

"Gimme one of those tortillas first." He grabbed the last one on the stove, singeing his fingers.

"Get away, get away," she said gruffly, but in mock anger only. She loved him to tease her this way. Stuffing a tortilla corner in his mouth, he said, "What's new, Ma?"

"Well then, I do have some news, but I'm not telling you until after supper."

"What's it about, Ma?"

"No. And why have you come so late?"

"I was hanging out at school." She needed to know everything. He saw the candle she kept burning in front of the picture of his father. "I was with Maggie."

"Ay, la mestiza?"

"Ma...."

"She'd never make you a good wife. She...."

"Who said anything about 'marry'?"

"Bueno, there is that, that she comes from a good family." Balestine was thinking about Doreen. What would his mother say about her if she knew his feelings?

"Are you going with her?" she was asking.

"Ma, we're just friends. Anyway, how the hell would I afford a wife?"

"No swearing," his mother admonished, making the sign of the cross. "Your mouth is getting too dirty. You should go more to church."

"What do you mean, dirty? Don't you like it? More like a man?" he kidded her, embracing her and kissing her cheeks.

"Sit down!" she ordered. But underneath, she was pleased. He was her boy and he showed no sign that he was in a hurry to leave her. Thanks to la Virgencita!

He ate everything she put on his plate. She noted it with satisfaction. But she worried that he never seemed to get fatter. Well, he was never sick either, thank God.

Balestine had forgotten about the news until she said, "I bet you'd never guess; they say they're going to give us pretty houses."

"What do you mean, give us pretty houses?"

"They're going to knock everything down here, but they're going to build us houses," she added quickly.

"What do you mean they're going to knock this down? Who told you?"

"The man came today. He told everybody, house by house, they're going to knock this down."

"They can't just knock down our houses, Ma!"

"Sí. Everything. Everybody, they're going to knock down. Everybody has to go."

"I don't want to go." He did not completely believe it yet. "How can they do that?"

"It is, how do you say it, it's urban renewal, la renovación de la ciudad. The city says we have to go and we have to. Why do you want to stay in this broken down place? Why?"

"Do you know where they're going to make us live? In some lousy apartamento with a hundred people up our ass!"

"Don't talk like that, mi hi'to." He rejected the idea of moving with fury and it frightened her.

"Ma, here at least we have our own house. They want to take away the last thing we have."

"This isn't a house. Freezing in the wintertime, boiling in the summer." She began to feel stubborn. "At least you boys can have your own room over there."

"Who said? They'll probably squash us all up together. And how are we going to pay for it? Did they tell you that?"

"They're going to be houses para los pobres, for the poor."

"Ma, they're not going to be free."

"No, if they make us move, they're going to have to pay for the house. Either for that house or for this one."

"Ma..." he gave up. "When do we have to go?"

"They're going to let us know by a paper. By mail."

He felt sick. "I'm gonna go sit by the river."

"Did you finish? But be careful, it's already dark."

He had to get outside. He needed air and the sky for what he was feeling. "Put the bar on the door, Ma."

"Bueno, anyway, Eddie will be home soon. And don't smoke too much."

He had not even thought of smoking. The Lucky Strike pack he had rolled up in the sleeve of his T-shirt was almost empty. He fingered it absently with his fingers. He looked back at the shack. The paper on the roof was beginning to lift again. He would have to fix things before he left. Why should it make any difference to him anyway if they moved; he was leaving. But it did matter. This was the place he wanted to come back to, damn it. This was really the only home they had known...playing along the banks of the rio since they were kids; dancing in the summer rains at the bottom of the riverbed; digging their toes into the muddy swirling water. They chased each other up and down the slippery banks until they were covered in mud and their mother had to wash them off with the hose. This shack on the rio under this sky was better than any welfare piece of shit apartamento. He said it to himself bitterly, but he could not help but see how it affected his mother. She was tired of all this. Tired of washing their clothes in a bandeja and heating the iron on a wood stove. She would have all the electricity she wanted. She deserved to have something in her life. But he wanted to give it to her. The Army would be a start. Maybe he could even be a career man, like they said. Be an officer and make a lot of money. He wanted to go, and he wanted to stay. He wanted to be someone else but he could not imagine it. The love and hate he felt for the place and for his life there were too much, and he threw himself down and gave himself to the sky.

Swirls of red cloud hung in the darkening sky. Wood smoke and sparks blew over his head. Supper smells and the sound of kids making noise before they settled down for bed. He couldn't imagine all this gone. This full-of-life place just cleared away. For what? So the gringos wouldn't be ashamed for the tourists to see the dirty Mexicans living in their shacks? They weren't free anymore. Their lives belonged more and more to the gringos, dependent on their generosity or their disdain. Everything they wanted to do they did, while people like him had to eat shit. It was because they were poor. That's what he came back to over and over.

"If we weren't poor we wouldn't be living here anyway," said Eddie when Bale told him the gringos were getting rid of La Milpa. *"We'd* be living in some new house in the desert—wasting tons of water to grow grass," he added with disgust. But Bale didn't care how it would be if they had money. Sure, his mother wouldn't have to worry so much, but it had to do with rights—he felt it like a lump in the gut. He couldn't throw it up or shit it out. He couldn't poke it with a stick and find out what kind of animal was eating his tripes from the inside. He had to swallow it and choke.

He slammed the door when he came back into the house. He was sick to death of the beautiful night and the sky. Sick of this lonely desert where there was no place to go to get away from it, no way to leave. Nothing to do but to keep eating his beans and tortillas with his mouth shut like a cow lying down. Everything he loved, the desert, the rio, his home and the food he ate was unbearable. It made him a prisoner even as it gave him life. More and more he could not find a happy moment anywhere.

Elmira was already lying down behind the blanket she used to separate her bed from the rest of the room. She wanted the boys to have the warm place by the fire.

"Ma, did you go to bed?" He wanted to let her know it was all right.

"I'm doing my prayers. Do you need something?"

"I don't need anything, Ma. Goodnight. Thanks for supper."

"Be sure to see to the fire before you fall asleep. Goodnight, my sons." She continued to pray. He heard the clicking of her beads. She prayed for the strength to take care of them, to raise them to be men. She prayed for the soul of Balestine, her husband, that he would come out quickly from purgatory. She prayed that God would illuminate her so she would know how to make Bale want to go to the new apartamentos. She prayed that he would finish school successfully and have a job with a good wage. And that he would find a good girl to take care of him and love him and they would be happy. For Eddie, she prayed that he would grow up soon before she should die, Dios mío. She reminded herself that he was bigger than Bale. So, satisfied that she had done everything for them with God, she went to sleep.

But Bale did not sleep. "How come you have to get so mad about everything?" said Eddie. "The men don't want to work La Milpa anymore anyway."

"They say that every year." But he knew it was true. Eddie didn't answer. He was content in the warm bed next to his brother. Bale lay on his back on top of the covers looking up at the ceiling. He saw spiders crawling around up there. "It'll be great," murmured Eddie. "Everybody was talking about it tonight. New houses. Who cares if they're apartamentos? They're gonna be *new*, man." Eddie fell asleep feeling freer than he had in a long time. The weight of poverty was not so heavy on his shoulders now. But Bale alone could not go to sleep. He was awake, stiff and uncomfortable. He lay in his misery, anger and loneliness. Against his will, he finally had to get under the covers because of the cold. Without taking off his clothes, and still shaking, he huddled next to Eddie and took what comfort he could get from the warmth of his brother. At long last, he fell into an uneasy sleep.

The fire burned out. A new moon shone high in the sky. The light of many stars glittered down through the desert night. And the coyotes howled in the hediondilla. But far to the northeast something grey and ugly which had lain hidden along the northern slopes uncurled and rose slowly into the night air. It rose and dissipated with the breezes of the night. If any had seen, maybe only a few gringos would have recognized what it was. Others would have taken it for something natural, something they did not yet know the words for. It was the first signs of air pollution, pressing against the flanks of the mountains and lifting on the winds. It was smog. In the hundreds of years this desert had taken to emerge from the.

swamplike homes of the first root and pod gatherers, there had never been any before.

Humans slept while the animals awakened and hunted for food. If there was something alien in the wind this night, it was brief. They continued to live their lives in the beauty and finality of the moment without knowing that this was the beginning of the end of their lives, their habitats, their world. For now, the desert and its life seemed endless; the delicate balance of vegetable and animal life undisturbed, eternal.

Chapter 20

▲

That year it was a very hot summer. The monsoon rains were late in coming. Earlier than usual, Grandmother had made her first batch of tes'win, a fermented native drink. And then she proposed they go look for chucata, a sap that came out on mesquite trees when it was very hot. She considered chucata a delicacy.

Mariana was sitting in the yard when Maggie drove up. At first she didn't notice, but Maggie pulled her over to the white Buick. "Remember? It was the Stones'. Grandmother's buying it. And today we're going out to the desert to find chucata." She was out of breath. Maggie dashed through the house getting things together for the trip. She got Mariana ready, handed her the straw hat and put her in the car. Then she drove carefully down the road and over the bridge and through El Barrio Central going the long way to the rancherías so Mariana could enjoy the ride. When they arrived at Grandmother's, Maggie put the top down, cautioning Grandmother to wear a scarf for the wind. The old woman grumbled about the ten dollars a month she was paying the Stones for this extravagance. But she only did it to hide her excitement. Maggie could tell she was pleased. She was glad she'd taken the driver's training course because now she could take them all to do something they enjoyed. Finally they were ready to go, Grandmother ensconced in the back seat, wearing her tapalo *and* a hat and surrounded by supplies. To Maggie's surprise, Mariana took out an ancient pair of sunglasses. She put them on with a flourish and made herself into a stylish woman. Maggie wore her western hat that matched the turquoise interior of the car. So they happily drove away from the rancherías taking El Camino del Rey west.

To get to where the mesquite was particularly dense, they had to follow the highway for several miles, take the old road over Colt's Pass to the valley and then strike out into the desert in the direction of the small peaks. It was only midmorning but the heat was intense, so Maggie pulled over after Colt's Pass and made the top go up on the car—much to the delight of the women. Maggie wondered if Grandmother was impressed with her facility around this mechanical thing, but she decided nothing like that could possibly impress her. Still, the glee visible on the old woman's wrinkled face made her happy. Maggie drove slowly towards the small peaks. When she was directly north of a certain wide gulch she turned the car south, navigating through flat dry desert.

Cacti were sparse. This was an area of tough crabgrass and palo verde. As they went south, ocotillo became interspersed with palo verde. It soon disappeared and mesquite took over. Just when Maggie was going to ask Grandmother for directions, she came around a stand of mesquite right up on a cattle fence. She drove the nose of the Buick up to the barbed wire and got out to see where it went. Grandmother got out too. She was afraid of having made a mistake in telling Maggie where to turn. She walked around catching sight of Colt's Pass and the peaks and decided, no, this was where she always came. Maggie leaned against one fender, working the brim of her hat. "Well, what do you want to do?"

"*Pues ya que estamos aquí, entramos.* Now that we're here, let's go in," said Grandmother.

"*Así pienso yo.* That's what I think." Maggie was glad she had thought to bring a knapsack and a blanket for everyone to sit on. She scouted out a place where the barbed wire was almost down, jumped over and held the wire for the others. Then Grandmother guided them through the mesquite. After examining a few trees, she said the chucata was ready.

The large crystalline drops that collect on mesquite bark when the weather is particularly warm is the tree crying, Grandmother said. Maggie decided she simply did not have the taste for it. And she didn't like how it stuck all over the inside of her mouth. Grandmother said that was because she didn't suck on it properly. Her own pleasure as she tore off the big chunks was evident. Maggie had to admit that eating some made the heat more tolerable. She looked around and saw Mariana delicately pushing aside some mesquite branches to reach the bark underneath. In an old pair of men's pants and a too-large shirt, her motions were still like a dance. She looked up and gave Maggie a slight smile of acknowledgement. Her face was bright when Maggie adjusted her mother's hat, then looked in her bag and congratulated her on her success. Mariana didn't speak but her features had lost the tight look she'd worn for so long.

Maggie danced over to Grandmother and shouted with exuberance, "We can do this all the time!" Grandmother was unsticking her skirt from the sharp thorns of a low-lying palo verde branch.

"Don't get excited," she said dryly and gave Maggie a little shove to move her aside. She bit off a piece of chucata from a chunk the size of her palm she had just gleaned and stood savoring it. She made sucking noises with her lips and tongue. Maggie was going to tease her about it when she suddenly heard the sound of a truck coming. An open-backed pickup tore up to them and stopped in a cloud of dust. A tall man, wearing western clothes, jumped out saying, "What are you people doing here? Habla English?" Before Maggie could answer, the Mexican clinging to the back called out, *"Dice que sí que hacen aquí.* He wants to know what you are doing here."

"I speak English," said Maggie. She pushed back her hat, showing her startling yellow hair. "We're just walking around looking for chucata."

"Didn't you see the fence? This is cattle country, private property." He eyed each of them in turn, his eyes stopping at Mariana.

"You *own* all this?"

"Same thing—leased it from the U.S. government for ninety-nine years. Yes, Ma'am, all four thousand acres of it. Got to have ten acres to every one steer, grazin's so poor." While he was talking he was moving closer to Mariana, ignoring the rest. Mariana was fanning herself slowly with her hat. Her dark wavy hair clung to her forehead, her cheeks were flushed. She looked younger and prettier than she had in years.

"I wouldn't want y'all to get in the way of a steer, now," he addressed Mariana, bending low to catch her eye. But Mariana, long lashes brushing her cheek, refused to look up or give any sign she'd heard.

"She...doesn't understand English," said Maggie quickly, stepping over to them. Just then Grandmother, who had been sitting on a rock, stood up and announced loudly in English, "We ben coming here for many years—chucata is good here!" Maggie was too surprised to say anything.

"Huh? What's she saying?" Maggie translated her English.

"Well, you people can't come here anymore." He was starting to get frustrated and impatient but still tried to be nice. "Just finish what you're doing—what is that stuff, anyway?—and don't cross a fence again. It means tres-passing. You know tres-pass-ing?" This last was directed at Grandmother, who smiled and nodded vigorously. "Come on, compadre," he waved the Mexican back on the truck, and still stealing curious looks at Mariana, jumped in and started the engine with a roar. The Mexican, hat in hand, hesitated and said, "*Lo siento mucho, Señora.* I'm very sorry." As he climbed up into the truck, his boss, the tall man said, "Don't they have their own reservation or something?" Maggie alone heard this last and she threw her pack down in disgust as the truck pulled out. She hated that tears came to her eyes. Grandmother stood unmoving, supporting herself with her stick, sucking her chucata and enjoying it.

"*Abuelita.* Grandmother…" Maggie began.

"*Ay! Un cerquito más o menos.* Huh. One small fence more or less." Grandmother spit through her teeth.

"It's trespassing. He *owns* all this."

"Then let's go," she said abruptly. She started walking quickly back the way they had come. Maggie was still standing there. "Shit!" she said and went to collect Mariana who had not moved an inch. Holding her mother by the hand and shouldering the knapsack, Maggie caught up to Grandmother at the fence. "I didn't mean we should just leave." The heat had gone out of her.

"Bueno. We'll sit in the car."

"No, it'll be too hot." Maggie saw a large old mesquite with overhanging branches a short distance away. There was enough shade for all of them. Pulling Mariana over to it and dumping her knapsack she said, "At least we won't have to hunt all over for the car." Grandmother with her stick under her arm spread out the blanket and sat down.

It was not yet noon. Under the mesquite a cool breeze fanned them as they rested. Maggie wanted to think but she was too churned up. She wanted to shout and swear but she was full of broken words that wouldn't come out. Mariana was napping; she didn't seem to care what happened. And Grandmother munched happily on her chucata and drank swallows of water from the jug. Then she pulled apart everything Maggie had packed and spread the lunch out in front of her. She spread some of her own homemade marmalade on a tortilla, rolled it up and began eating.

Maggie watched in disbelief. "Grandmother, aren't you mad at that jerk?" she began, but Grandmother interrupted her in Spanish.

"I'm on my way down," she said cheerfully. "Now you must figure things out." She was chewing her tortilla and marmalade with satisfaction. "Here, eat something."

"I'm not hungry," Maggie muttered. She was a kettle of seething emotions. She rolled up a tortilla and started eating it dry. The clear bright blue of the sky fell as flashing slivers through the mesquite branches.

"Grandmother," she began when she could trust her voice. "Why did you speak to that man in English?"

"So he didn't think we were just savages here."

"But you've never cared what anyone thought before."

"The world is changing."

"Well, I'm not going to be in this one on their terms."

"Those who don't tighten their belts will not be in this world at all," Grandmother said simply. Maggie started to argue but Grandmother said, "Now I'm tired. You study it well." And with that final word she arranged herself on the blanket and covered her face with her pañuelo. Maggie lunged off in the direction of a small hill.

Grandmother caring what that ignorant jerk thought —how could she? The picture of the old woman standing there in her long black skirt and dusty, wornout shoes speaking English to a gringo that wouldn't understand her even if he could, and furthermore didn't care, made her want to throw up. She wanted to punch the guy in the face and squirrel Grandmother away where no one would see her or hurt her feelings. But why should she? "This is our desert, damn it! Our desert! How could anyone own it?" After her anger and incredulity she felt an overwhelming sadness. Where would they go? What would they do? What would happen to them? For the first time, she fully understood Balestine's despair. At the same time, she couldn't give up. She had to think it through carefully, and do it in English. So maybe Grandmother had been right in making her speak it. God, I just don't know, she thought. She walked up on a small rise where she could see out over the valley and sat down on a rock. She tried to put the spirit of this place inside of her, somehow contain it with her body, but it was too late. It was already lost to her. The harder she tried to keep things the way they had always been, the faster they seemed to slip away.

When she came back, she found the two women sitting in the car. "Well, we found lots of chucata," Grandmother said agreeably on the way home. Maggie glanced at Mariana and saw she was smiling. She smiled back. For so long Mariana had been going farther away and now she was coming back. Maggie stopped trying to understand everything. By the time they reached the ranchería, she was almost peaceful. She fed the chickens, then carried some wood in for Grandmother. She applied herself to the simple chores. She was safe in feelings and motions she understood—arranging kindling, taking pleasure in the scent of flowers and the simple companionship of the night. The clarity of the world lay in the sight of the old woman sitting in her favorite chair. Maggie had not really looked at the yard in a long time. The wild roses were growing beautifully. The sour oranges Grandmother made her marmalade from were lush and lovely on the tree.

The three women sat side by side on the patio. From there they could see all the way south. The alfalfa was stacked in bales in the Quatillo's fields. One corner of the house could be seen, bright white. They could see all the way to the mountains, pink and gold and dotted with sage. On impulse Maggie leaned over and pressed her cheek against Grandmother's. "Someday," the words caught in her throat, "I'm going to buy you all the shoes in the world."

"*Quita, quita.* Get away," said Grandmother, but she gently patted Maggie's hand. Driving home to Mariana's, Maggie had wanted to laugh remembering Grandmother and the events of the day. But she had wanted to cry too.

While Mariana was lying down, Maggie hooked up the pump to the generator, got the hose and started the water running to wash the car. It was a luxury, but she thought that this once Grandmother would approve. From then on it would be buckets from the trough, she told herself. She washed the car with soap and scrubbed the tires and then the chrome with Ajax. Then she got a little gun oil, stretched it out with Crisco and went over the whole car with a rag. It wasn't quite like that stuff, oil of a turtle, but the car was cleaned and protected. Tomorrow she would take care of the interior. She leaned back against a fender, carefully, and contemplated the woodpile. As tired as she felt, she still went and got the axe and started breaking a few sticks. She wanted to get the last of the unrest out so she could think. She was still breaking wood when Frank drove up in his Studebaker. He barely glanced at Maggie as he staggered into the house.

Chapter 21

▲

Maggie finished chopping wood and then debated whether to go into the house or not. She had heard no sound coming from there. Suddenly she broke her stance and ran to the door, almost stepping on a chick pecking its way around the porch. She flung open the door.

Mariana had been lighting a fire; a piece of kindling was still in her hand. Smoke was coming from the stove where the new flame was dying unfed. She was bent almost double under the weight of Frank's hands. He was shaking her so hard the spit flew from her mouth. Just as Maggie entered the room, the piece of kindling dropped from Mariana's hand, but she didn't utter a sound.

"What are you doing to her?" Maggie screamed.

"We are having a conversation," Frank said through his teeth, "a very pri-vate conversation." He kept shaking Mariana while twisting his head to take in Maggie with bloodshot eyes. Maggie started towards him. "Take your hands off her!"

"Hey, she knows what to do: just give me the money."

"There's no money," Maggie pleaded. "There isn't anything...."

"Yeah?" he broke in, "well whose car zat I saw outside, the neighbor's?" He pronounced each word succinctly with slurring emphasis.

"Let her go!" Maggie was no longer pleading. She took another step forward, not thinking about what she would do. She saw Mariana reach up a hand in slow motion and dig her nails into the flesh of Frank's forearm. More shocked than hurt, he swore and let her drop to the floor.

"Mama!"

He turned his full gaze on Maggie then and she saw real hatred in his eyes. "*You're* teachin' her that, aren't you, bitch? Always coming between us!" He took a step toward her. And another step, reaching out for her with two massive hands.

"*You* did! *You* came between you!" she cried. There was no time but she was already diving for the bed, fingers reaching underneath for the box, knocking it away from the gun that was in her hand. His mouth fell open and that second of indecision gave her time to slam a bullet into the chamber. Her thumb pulled back the hammer as she spoke, the words bursting free from her mouth: "If you ever touch her again, if you ever touch either of us again, I'll blow your guts out!"

"Wha..wha..you'd take *my* gun, the beautiful gun *I* gave you...? Ha, ha, ha," he said, swaying in her direction. Maggie stood her ground and the gun never moved. Her eyes were like burning slits. He broke before her. "Ha, ha," he said, groping for the door, swinging it open so hard it smacked against the wall. He backed out, curling his lip at her and slammed the door shut. She heard him gunning the engine of his car and experienced a moment of panic thinking he might ram the house, but she heard him drive away, the car scattering gravel and raising a cloud of dust that took minutes to fade from the window. The sound of the motor faded away too, but it was more moments still before Maggie realized how hard she was clenching the gun. She released the pressure of her finger on the trigger. Her heart was pounding when she let the gun drop on the bed and ran to Mariana.

Holding each other, they ran outside. The dust was settling in the bend in the road. Half crying and half laughing, Maggie opened the door to the Buick and they both got in. "Wait a minute," she said, and made the top go down. Then they sat quietly inside the car just breathing and looking out at the sky. Maggie realized that her mother was still crying, but after a while she wiped her eyes and Maggie felt a hand pat her gently on the head the way Grandmother did it. "Yes," Maggie responded. To the east they saw the peak of La Madre shining like a rose in the light of the evening sun. "Yes," Maggie sighed. "Yes."

El Cuento:

Había una vez una cierva hermosa. Era grande e inteligente y les enseñó a sus hijos cómo huir de los cazadores. Trataron de hallarla para matarla porque mientras ella estaba viva, no iban a tener buena caza. Pero nunca la pudieron agarrar. Cuando se pusieron alrededor del monte donde estaba, se quedaba en su nido. Cuando mandaron los perros atrás de ella, puso salvia por todo el camino y se perdieron. Vivió mucho tiempo la cierva y llegó el día en que se le hizo pesada la vida. Se quiso morir y se presentó a los cazadores pero ellos se dijeron unos a otros, ya está de mucha edad la cierva y no va a ser buena para comer. Entonces no la quisieron matar. De modo que esperó muchos años a que viniera La Muerte pero su espera fue inútil. Al fin, comprendió. Se ofreció a la oscuridad dicendo, "Me hago como tú," y murió.

The Story:

Once there was a beautiful deer. She was large and intelligent and taught her sons how to evade the hunters. They tried to find her and kill her because as long as she was alive there was no good hunting. But they never could catch her. When they surrounded the hillside she was on, she stayed in her nest. When they sent dogs after her she spread the trail with sage and they got lost. The deer lived a long time and then one day life became a burden to her. She wanted to die and presented herself to the hunters, but they said to one another, "She's old and no good to eat," so they wouldn't kill her. She waited many years in vain for death to come. At last, she understood. She offered herself to the twilight, saying, "I make myself like you," and she died.

Chapter 22

▲

"What are you doing tonight?"

"Nothing. And you?"

"Nada. Wanna hang out with me, half-breed?"

"That depends, cholo."

"We'll go anywhere you want to go." Bale lifted his eyebrows, serious. "Eddie'll come too, okay?"

"Sure. It's Friday night, right? There's not too many left for him," she teased Eddie.

"Don't give him bad luck," Bale protested.

"Hey! I can take care of myself." Bale slapped Eddie affectionately on the cheek in answer. "Okay, so let's go." Maggie gave Eddie the rest of her hamburger and he wolfed it on the way to the door.

"Kid's always growing!" Bale nodded at Eddie. It was Friday night and school was a long way off again. They put the top down in Bale's Ford, laughing and kidding each other. It was a wonderful warm night. When they reached the Spanish Trail, Maggie said, "Go north, okay?" She still felt uneasy about the mountains to the east and she wanted this to be a totally frivolous night. Bale amiably turned the car north and Maggie and Eddie leaned back, revelling in the flood of stars.

"You can really see the sky from out here," Maggie said.

"Yeah." Eddie was dazzled by three shooting stars in succession. It had to mean a lucky omen for the Brahmas. But the stars were gone before he could wish for anything. They drove well off the main roads, meandering from one car track to another, getting deeper into the desert. Finally Bale stopped and turned off the lights. They sat for a few moments in silence, just looking at the beauty of the stars. "So many worlds," said Maggie. She got out and walked a little ways; she wanted to be surrounded by the soft glow of the desert. The desert was alive with sound: crickets singing with all their might. Recent rains filled the air with sage. She breathed deeply. She came back to the car as Bale was breaking open a couple of beers. The bitter cold taste made her remember the time with Grandmother in Baja when she was a kid, waiting for the boats to come in, the fishermen dropping gunny sacks of clams on the beach as the last stars were disappearing. She took another swallow and remembered cracking clams and squeezing lime juice on them and washing down the morsels with a swallow of beer. The early morning, bright and specific, the cliffs white, the palm leaves on the cabaña lifting with the sea breeze...She heard Eddie saying, "Where did you get this?"

"From the Trocadero, from Fernando," said Bale. Maggie knew Bale's cousin worked at the midway point to the border, and he was always into one deal or another.

"Mexican beer is great," she said.

"Any beer is great," said Eddie, chugging the last drops from his bottle. "Is there any more?"

"Yeah, but not for you," said his brother.

"If I'm old enough to fight the Brahmas, I'm old enough for beer."

"Who said you were old enough? Crazy enough, maybe."

"You can finish mine," said Maggie. She flipped on the radio, searching along the band. "I want you two to hear something. Listen to this." *Devil or angel, I can't make up my mind*... The song came in loud and clear. "This is Chicago!"

"Chicago?" they exclaimed.

"Yeah. I found it one night when I was driving around in the desert. You can only pick it up way out here, late at night." They listened to the song and to the distance, each in his own thoughts. They felt so small, in the middle of nowhere, being sung to from a grand city many miles and worlds away.

"Someday I'm gonna go there," said Eddie from the back seat.

"What the hell for?" Bale shut the radio off.

"Whadda you mean? To see what it's like!"

Bale started the engine. They didn't care where they went, watching the cactus moving towards them slowly out of the dark. Eddie was thinking about big American cities, cars and skyscrapers, and *girls* walking on high high heels down the avenues. Girls swinging their hips. He closed his eyes and then opened them fast, a little dizzy.

"Let's go to La Guadalupe." Maggie thought of it suddenly. She thought of the walls covered by paintings and all the other beautiful things made from the desert. "We'll be able to see the moon from inside through one of the skylights."

They found the right road by the crepe paper streamers tied to some cholla, red and green waving in the breeze. The Yaquis always decorated the trail for midnight Mass on Christmas Eve, and the decorations stayed on all year.

They left the car at the end of the road and walked up the gently curving trail through an empty corral to the adobe walls. Standing in the entrance of the building dedicated to her, they could see La Guadalupe illuminated by countless candles burning in veladoras. They walked up to her image in silence while Maggie searched for a dime to put in the offering plate. Then she found a wick and lit a candle. After saying a prayer they spread out, each on his own, investigating the various rooms. Each of the walls was different, painted with scenes of the Indios and the desert, simple figures and bright colors. The floors were set with the warm colors of stones taken in their natural state from the desert. The small windows were covered with shutters made from saguaro ribs, grey and weathered.

She found the tiny room she liked the most. Part of the skylight was decorated with pieces of colored glass. The starry sky shone down through the opening. A large tumbleweed hung upside down from the ceiling with desert stones inside it hanging from invisible threads. Maggie sat against the wall where she could see a patchwork of stars. She wished this was her home. She wished that she could be the artist who had made this beautiful place. She wanted a home that was like this. In such a place she would not feel a stranger. She would be where her life made sense. She felt these thoughts not with words but with her spirit.

Eddie came in and lay down on the floor, Bale sat against the wall beside her. Legs stretched out in front of them, they gazed up at the stars. A soft sweet sound came from another room. "Chimes!" said Maggie.

"It's nice here," Eddie murmured. He was warm and strangely peaceful. He no longer felt all disarranged, like his limbs were too big for his body. He didn't feel like his brother's shadow.

"Do you come here a lot?" Bale asked.

"Sometimes. I used to, but not lately."

"With guys?"

"No. I mean, a guy I knew brought me here once and then I came back myself."

"How come? I mean, how come by yourself?"

"I don't know. I always felt like I was acting...and then Frank always wanted to know everything, so...I just made up my mind one day not to go out on any more dates."

"Were your folks mean or what?"

"Frank...Frank was crazy."

"What did he do?"

"I don't want to talk about it."

"Okay."

"What about yours?"

Bale looked over at Eddie, who seemed to be asleep. He zipped up his jacket. "My ma tells everybody my father died in the war. She doesn't want anybody to think we've been starving."

"What happened to him?"

"He was on his way. I mean, they had come from las estaciones to the recruiting place in El Pueblo to get sworn in. They must have been in a big hurry. They said he was hanging his head out the window, looking at the town when the bus missed a curve and turned over. He must have been pretty messed up—they wouldn't let us see him. When my mother took his clothes down to the funeral parlor, they just shook their heads. But she left them anyway. He wasn't legally in the Army yet, so all they gave us was the funeral. He was in a sealed casket. We never saw him again. That's all I remember. I must have been about three or four."

"They should have given you something."

"We didn't have the money to fight. He was the only one killed. They made it sound like it was his fault."

"They didn't have to do that with my stepfather. It *was* his fault."

"Yeah?"

"Frank was drunk, that's all. He went off the road near Cascaron. He had a woman over there. I guess he was going to her. Anyway, the car hit some rocks and burned. Se hizo chicharrón." Maggie laughed and Bale burst out laughing too. "They shoulda just raked what was left under a mesquite. We were glad he was never coming back."

"Yeah, we wondered what happened."

"He used to hit my mother all the time. And me. That's why Mama's the way she is, sort of not all there. Don't tell anybody what I said, okay?"

"Don't worry. Who the hell would I tell?"

"You know, like Doreen."

"I don't tell her anything of family business."

"So anyway, after that Mama *smiled.* I think at first she couldn't believe he wasn't going to walk through that door any minute. And then maybe she felt it was a sin to be glad. But I can say it—I'm glad he's gone. I'm glad he died, because if he hadn't, I think I might have killed him myself."

"That bad, huh?"

"Yeah."

Neither one said anything more for awhile. Maggie put her head back and saw a shooting star. She felt like it was for her. "Sometimes I want to spill my guts out to the whole world—it seems like all we were taught was to hide everything—and then sometimes I don't want anybody to know anything. You know?"

"Maybe we were taught to hide because everything in our lives *is* shit, especially being poor."

"Yeah, but then we are ashamed of *hiding* too! You know? Now I can't get rid of all the shame I feel. I mean, it's bad enough to have the problems we have. That's why I never want to talk about it. Like the counselors at school. They always asked all these questions about my family. Why didn't they ask me if I wanted to go to college? When Frank died, at first we missed just the little he had brought. I heard there was some money to help kids out. When I asked about it, the guy looked at me and said it was for *really poor* kids."

"First they want us to look one way, and then another," said Bale.

"I used to wash my blouse and skirt out every night and iron it the next morning," Maggie explained. "You know, they make it so no matter what we do, it's the wrong thing."

Bale laughed. "Maybe we should spit on a rattlesnake and let her bury the shit in the ground."

"Yeah, right, I wish it was so easy...but anyway, a couple months later I went to work at Penney's."

"I was just thinking about my mother. When I was real little I used to think it was really neat sleeping on the floor, but one day I caught her crying and she told me it was her wedding furniture she had sold to eat." He paused. "That was all she had, you know? I don't really remember, but I know we had a little ranchería near the border with chickens, but we lost it." He told her about the urban renewal stuff then. "To them, we're just a pile of garbage, an embarrassing crap on the edge of their nice town. They don't think that it means something to us."

"It hurts to see everything ending, doesn't it?"

"Yeah, it hurts like hell. It's welfare, Maggie. It's like prison."

"What about everybody else?"

"You mean, besides me? That's what Eddie says. Maybe I'm the only one that cares, but I think as soon as people hear they can't do anything about it, they stop thinking about what they really want."

"It's progress," said Maggie. "When I was a little kid I heard people talking about it all the time—and wanting it—to them progress meant highways. You can't imagine how excited people got about a highway coming in because it meant more commerce could take place. That's how it was in Mexico too. Progress meant pasteurized milk and doctors. It meant pushing back the snakes and scorpions. I mean, it's great in theory, but who can afford doctors anyway? Around here everybody went to the huesero in the Barrio. Or to my nina.

"But you know, as great as things were for the kids, running all over the fields and canals down in Baja, everybody that wasn't busy working would run and gather around any car driving in! It was contact with the outside world. The life of the city, which everyone thought had to be great."

Bale was serious again. "So, if they leave us alone, what do we do when we're too big to play in the fields and canals?"

"Yeah, that's a whole other problem. The way it is, we're just dependent on what the gringos give us. And this is what happens," said Maggie.

"But what's it going to be like for the viejitos? What are they going to do when they have to walk miles in the hot sun to buy their food at the grocery store? All the americanos have cars. What do they know about walking miles to get something a penny cheaper, because it's necessary?"

"I don't know. For Grandmother, progress means the end of her world and her existence here...."

"Do you know something? I hate the new roads here. They just mean more houses for the americanos and more of the desert gone. Houses for them—those are the pretty houses my ma talks about, not what they're going to give us."

"But if they were houses for us, would that make it different?"

"Okay, okay, it's not the houses, it's...it's..." It was too hard for him to talk anymore. Maggie tried to comfort him. "Maybe it won't be as bad as you think...." But she saw his face.

"I'd rather be dead than live in one of those," he said.

"Come on, Bale. At least the families will be together. No more wondering if you're going to slide into El Río in a bad rain. No more tourists gaping at you from the bridge." The smallest smile played at the corners of his mouth.

"When we were little we used to go out at night with flashlights, even in the rain, and look for the centavos they threw from the bridge."

"What did you do with the money?"

"It wasn't much, just pennies and sometimes a nickle. We'd go to the balcony of the State and throw popcorn down on the big kids. And then run all over the theater."

"And stick Bazooka under the seats, I bet."

"Me? Never!" he grinned. He was glad they were here. He felt like he could just go to sleep. He yawned. "I wish we could stay here and get up in the morning and make chorizo and eggs...."

"...and saddle the horses," said Maggie.

"What horses?" Eddie was stretching with a sleepy frown on his face. "What are you guys talking about?"

"Look who's waking up," Maggie teased him.

"I wasn't asleep."

"What do you mean—you were waking the dead with your snores," said Bale.

"Come on, you guys."

"Hey, let's go play hide 'n seek now that Eddie's awake," said Maggie.

"That kid's game?" scoffed Eddie.

"It's not such a kid's game out here in the dark."

"Yeah," Bale added, "wait 'till some esqueleto grabs your balls from behind."

"Aw, come on." Eddie was too embarrassed to look at Maggie.

Later, the three of them stood outside looking up at the moon. It was only half full but shining brightly in the east. The hills were dark shapes. They felt the fullness of the desert, the sweet smells on the breeze. There was a harmony of integrated sounds, none of them human: crickets, mesquite branches brushing against one another, an occasional rock sliding, trickles of sand falling.

"Listen," Bale said to Maggie. "The night of the bulls, I have to meet Fernando at the Trocadero and bring him back to El Pueblo. He might be real late; can you drive down and bring the kid back?"

"Sure, I can't come 'till later anyway."

"Yeah, and I can practice driving too," said Eddie.

"You might be too out of it," said Bale. "Don't forget, we're going to celebrate. You'll come with us, okay?" he said to Maggie. "We'll go to my uncle Hilberto's. We can dance and drink some beer and sing. We'll make some memories. It'll be great."

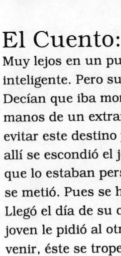

El Cuento:

Muy lejos en un pueblito había un joven muy
inteligente. Pero su destino no era bueno.
Decían que iba morir a los quince años a
manos de un extraño. Sus padres quisieron
evitar este destino y buscaron una cueva y
allí se escondió el joven. Entonces vino uno al
que lo estaban persiguiendo y halló la cueva y
se metió. Pues se hicieron amigos los dos.
Llegó el día de su cumpleaños y ese día el
joven le pidió al otro que trajera su lanza y al
venir, éste se tropezó y clavó la lanza en el
joven. Cuando llegaron sus padres ya lo halla-
ron muerto el puro día que cumplió los
quince años.

The Story:

Far away there was a small village and there lived a young boy who was very intelligent. But his destiny was not good. They said he would die at the age of fifteen years at the hand of a stranger. His parents wanted to avoid this destiny and they looked for a cave and hid the boy there. Then another young man came along who was being followed and he found the cave and went in. Well, the two boys became friends. The day of his birthday arrived and that day the boy asked the other to bring his spear. As this one was coming, he stumbled and the spear went right into the young boy. When his parents arrived they found him dead—the exact day he was fifteen years old.

Chapter 23

▲

After spending Sunday morning with Mariana, Maggie had driven across the border into Mexico in time for Eddie's debut with the Brahmas. The afternoon had passed in a wave of excitement. That evening the three friends walked through the streets enjoying the long way to Hilberto's nightclub where they planned to celebrate the day. There was a chill in the night air but the mood of the crowd, so long confined by winter, was warm, exuberant. Above the town, patches of snow were still visible in the shadows among the pink and blue and yellow shacks hanging on the side of the hill. People were seeking pleasure now in the same way they had huddled together in introspection or penance before—with a largess of spirit, a fullness of the heart and an innocent expectation that life was good and joy would last.

Maggie, Balestine and Eddie made their way through the crowds of turistas and locals. Carefully shaven, well-dressed, smooth-talking men addressed the sightseers from the doorways of their establishments, exhorting them to enter. In the nightclubs, high-breasted women sat with crossed legs on the edges of barstools, smiling invitations to enjoy the pleasures of the night.

More than one man, seeing the color of Maggie's hair, called to her in English. Sometimes she answered, in Spanish, or simply smiled. A few more perceptive than the others switched to Spanish or spoke carefully to Balestine, her escort, her owner. Bale caught her eye and shrugged. But she saw a need in him to have that part of a woman she wanted to keep to herself, had never wanted to give to anyone. It would have been easy to allow herself to be protected by him, but she would not give in to what was expected of her. Although she would not have been able to name it, she wanted her own life. She was trying to think about this when she stumbled from the curb. She looked and saw the sidewalk had ended and the refuse-strewn, potholed street had begun. There was a legless beggar on a small wooden platform propelled by skates pushing his trunk along. He gestured to her in greeting and laughed, sharing in the life of the streets. She wondered if life like that was beautiful or cruel or ludicrous. Then she heard Eddie shout at her over the noise of the people and, looking up, she saw the neon of "Nightclub" in brilliant blue cursive.

The club appealed to americanos. Many were drinking and listening to the music of the band; a mariachi sound —a mixture of trumpets and violins—had been added to the usual drums and guitars, but in good taste, not too loud, not too fast. Eddie drank his beer, grinning from ear to ear. He had faced the Brahmas that afternoon and he was alive! The bull in the ways of his breed had tried to gore him any way he could, even trying to crush the boy against the barricade with his massive body. A Brahma did not charge true, but Eddie had made him come at him twice and he had passed him twice with the large muleta. The animal had swung his head around at the last minute, blowing his target's scent from flaring nostrils, searching with horns for his legs. And then it was over and everyone cheered wildly, throwing their hats in the air, and he had run into the embrace of his brother while the Brahma was still stabbing the barricade, venting his anger against the splintered wood.

Suddenly Eddie felt like he was burning up. He was sweating and all he wanted to do was put his head under cold water. He staggered to the men's room and when he didn't return, Bale went after him. "*Se le soltó el miedo. His fear got loose,*" Bale said to Maggie when he came back. "He didn't know how scared he was until he sat down."

"Why is he doing it?" Maggie wanted an easy explanation. She saw that she faced the same kind of choice Eddie had made. He had wanted to do something other than the expected: more than finding a girl, getting married, settling down. But if he didn't do that, he had to prove he was still a man, even more than just a man. So he fought the bulls. Eddie wanted another way, too, she thought. Bale was a brave one, willing to love, but just doing that was not enough for her. She wanted more than that. The women in the culture either ran loose or were over-sheltered, forced to be an ideal with no freedom to search for their own expression, passed from father to husband. Bale didn't think about those things, she saw.

Eddie came back a little green, but his uncle Hilberto had him by the arm. Hilberto was the perfect host, pouring a copa for each of them from the special bottle he carried. "*Para él que se hizo hombre!* For the one who made himself a man!" Hilberto announced for all to hear. Everyone toasted Eddie. Then Hilberto invited the three of them to go "in back" and they followed him, carrying their copas with them.

They went through a high-ceilinged room that was evidently a personal kitchen. An aging woman dressed in the Michoacan style stood over a stove. Her long grey hair in a braid, she was stirring what smelled like beans with a wooden spoon and keeping watch over a small child at the same time. She did not turn in their direction, but the child playing at her feet stared at Maggie, very seriously holding out a toy car with missing front wheels for her inspection. Maggie stopped to say something to him, but he backed away shyly. They passed through a pasillo, a corridor common in joining two houses, and entered another room. Hilberto closed the door carefully and seated them at an ornate table, carved and polished and glowing softly. Traditional paintings of Aztec men and women tastefully covered the walls illuminated by elegant track lights. The chairs they sat on were upholstered in black velvet. This room was only for guests, set aside in the custom of all Mexicans as a special room for intimate gatherings. A fresh bottle of primo tequila was introduced and a copa poured for all. They drank and relaxed, talking quietly.

Maggie watched Eddie and Bale talking about the Brahmas. Eddie was getting on top of the experience and already thinking about the next time. Courage suited him, Maggie thought, watching his shining eyes. Time passed in friendship and then Hilberto picked up two guitars which he offered to them. He himself played a guitarron. He set the base line to a fast corrido and they sang songs—of country, of justice and of lovers. When it was handed to her, Maggie accepted a guitar without hesitation. She strummed a few chords to find the right key and

then played something she had been fooling around with.
Her hands were strong and she played easily. It was a slow
ballad with a syncopated beat and there were no questions in her fingers about who or what she was; no
barriers to the music of her soul. Hilberto played with
feeling and Eddie picked out some melody notes that hung
beautifully in the air like silver light. No one was afraid of
the emotion of the music. Maggie invented new words and
lines and then another voice joined them, singing,

"*Juntos andamos dentro lumbre y llama...*

We go together between fire and flames,

on a journey demanded by the heart..."

A woman sang the words to the music Maggie had
created and she heard them with her blood. The woman
stood in the shadows of the entrance, her hand on her
hip, waiting. Hilberto went to her and she accepted his
invitation to enter the room with a dancing movement.
Now the spirit of communion at the table was complete.
The woman smiled at all of them and they came together
in one heart. Maggie fell into the emotion of the moment,
into the dream meaning of the words they sang, into a
world she had not absorbed before. She existed on an edge
of total clarity. The knowledge of the flesh spoke in
striking color and intensity and passion. She could not
endure it for long and, restless, she went where she could
watch the others, their shapes, their sounds mixing up
with the candlelight. Inside, she was tangled up in black
and gold. She was coming apart and coming together
again in the dark and liquid fissures of her body; joy was
pulling her muscles open, tendons separating from the
bones. Suddenly her ribcage was parted and her heart
was lifted high in a shower of blood. She was breathing
so hard she couldn't move and then the woman was by
her side, close to her with a calming arm around her
shoulders and she gasped for air and then everything was

okay again. She leaned against the wall and the woman said tenderly, "Why do you destroy your body to elevate your soul? Porqué, linda?" The tears already in Maggie's eyes ran down her cheeks. She couldn't stop them and she couldn't speak. Still holding her, the woman spoke gently, "It will not be forever like this, you'll see." The tone and certainty of the woman's voice brought truth to her body. She felt it unformed and yet to appear, but truth. She was very tired. She wanted to rest her head on the woman's breast. To shelter there in the other's knowledge.

"Hey, Gypsy," Hilberto was saying, "what tales are you weaving for this young girl?" The woman was talking to Maggie alone in words no one else could hear.

"*Cosas de mujer*. Things belonging to woman," she answered. Maggie was trying to grasp the words when the woman opened the door and, brushing against her, left the room.

"That one walks in whatever world she wants!" said Hilberto. He spoke with affection but also with longing. Maggie had not moved from her place against the wall. This woman had looked into her secret, creative heart and then she had left at a moment of her own choosing. Maggie had put out her hand to stop her, had looked for the right words to say but didn't know them. She had wanted to answer back the way she had been spoken to. The strength of what she wanted was there in her fingers on the other's hand. The woman had responded with a slight pressure, an acknowledgement, a promise. And then she had gone.

In the bathroom Maggie washed her face with cold water from the one working faucet. She didn't look at herself in the mirror. She was trying to remember all the words the woman had said but she felt like she was burning with fever. The more she tried to think everything out, the less she remembered. But the truth that all of them had been talking about and singing about was there, curled up in her stomach and wrapped around the excited beating of her heart. Her heart that no longer felt so fragile or so young. It would never feel that way again.

Chapter 24

▲

Maggie knew a place where they could go for café. It was on one of the crooked rocky streets on the south edge of town. Stepping over piles of rocks, they found the doorway to a tortilla factory that was open all night long. It was hard to see at first because of the darkness and the fires. There were several rows of comales and women kneeling in front of each one, slapping out round thick corn tortillas and cooking them on the hot irons. They went to the back of the room and seated themselves at a simple wooden table and waited. After a while they were given strong mexican coffee in big ceramic cups. A plate of tortillas was placed on the table before them. They thanked the woman who served them. They sipped the coffee and ate the sweet-smelling corn tortillas and looked at the women toiling in front of the fires.

Now they were serio, quiet and serious, because they had come from a room of luxury and here people were anonymous and laboring. Now Maggie saw her freedom. She acknowledged to herself that it was her mixed heritage that made her the one being served instead of the one squatting in front of the comal.

The whites were committing injustices against her people, against Grandmother's people, against the desert and the mountains. They were taking away the wildness. They made only logical decisions that crushed the feeling needs of others. This was how they made progress. This was how they ate the face of the earth.

Maggie wanted to tear the white blood out of herself. She wanted to sink into her dark blood and there within the Mother to bare her fangs and stand. But she did not have the choice of being all one thing. No matter how it hurt, she would never have that choice.

Maggie saw the fires blaze in the comales and in that burning she knew that the ignorance had been burned and disciplined from her own body by the fires of the earth. She remembered the woman at the nightclub saying, "It is a very confusing world out there. We must go on tiptoes to know what death is and what it is to be alive." She had nodded in Bale's direction. "We cannot play with death because death does not know how to play for fun."

Maggie understood and felt her mind walk on bare feet within the circle of the sacred place. She turned and saw that there had always been only one choice for her. She had to choose to be of mixed blood, to be both things. She had to be willing to accept this tension as a part of her being. By knowing this, she had already made her choice. A howl burst from the animal in her heart, but the voice that would speak was neither a scream nor a growl. Suddenly she felt the accumulation of emotion that had begun at the nightclub come out of her with a prophetic surge of power. She had seen the shadow at Bale's feet, and now, here it was, closer, leaning towards him and lapping at his very breath. She tried to say something to him, to warn him, but he had already turned away, laughing at something Eddie had said and it was too late.

She had come back to herself, back to a familiar room. She told herself she did not make sense, that she would go crazy if she wasn't careful. She told herself she was actually in a very civilized room with friends. It had been an intense day with the Brahmas and a happy night. They had drunk a couple of drinks and sung songs of joy and had the fun they wanted to have. But now it was finished and they would go back to life as it was before.

Chapter 25

The rider is coming to a meeting with the demands of his own spirit. Galloping in from the northwest, his finely pointed boots tight against fancy stirrups, he rides in absolute harmony with the moonlit world around him. Absorbed in the movement of leather against leather, he labors as the Great White Horse labors, breath for breath.

All that can really be seen is the shifting of shadow among silver cacti. All that can be heard is the rushing of wind through narrow canyons and the scratching of giant tumbleweeds rolling among the rocks of a deep ravine. The music of the night is made of distant rolls of thunder and the smells of rain and dust: the many mouths of the desert are opening to the coming sweep of rain.

The rider is ahead of the storm, hungry heart answering the call from another world. He does not know fear or the meaning of time. His being conforms itself to fragmen-

tary rock, to the rhythm of verticals, chasms and cross-
ings sounding notes in the wind. Other creatures have
already sought shelter from the storm. The coyote with a
final challenge of lifted snout to the darkness of the north
has curled up in her burrow among the roots of mesquite.
Nose to her tail, she warms herself with animal patience.
Scorpions skitter from rock to rock; one finally pulling a
rocky shelf over its head sits facing the glimmer of light
that still reaches into its miniscule chasm. Only an ant
or two, signals crossed by the wind, still struggle to regain
their holes. But these creatures have to do with life and
death, with the circumscription of prayers, and not with
other dimensions.

Chapter 26

▲

Speaking against the wind, Bale said to Eddie, "She's gonna drive, okay?" Eddie was too tired to object. In the cold, they walked as quickly as they could to the car. The streets were empty. Only a shopkeeper was sweeping the sidewalk in front of his establishment before locking the doors.

"I'm going to get Fernando at the Trocadero. I'll see you at home." Bale waved to them. He was driving away before Maggie had warmed up the engine of the Buick. She drove slowly to the border crossing. La migra took his time coming out from his warm building. He hunched his shoulders against the freezing wind that was blowing at him from the hills. They showed their passports and he asked the usual questions about what they were doing in Mexico and what they were bringing back. He stuck his head in the Buick, looked around, and then waved them on. He was already back inside before they had left the driveway. Maggie adjusted the heater and snapped up her jacket. Eddie was barely awake when she pulled onto the highway.

The road was very dark; only an occasional straggler returning to Mexico at this time of night showed his lights. Between la migra and the Trocadero there was nothing but desert for many miles. Tumbleweeds and brush blew frequently across the road so Maggie drove slowly and looked for some rock 'n roll on the radio to keep her awake. She found an all-night station out of El Pueblo playing soul. It cut in and out from the wind interference, but she hummed along to something by the Chantelles as they passed a windbreak of tamarack trees. Next to it was a stretch of barbed wire with a few steers huddled up together against the wire. After they passed the tamarack the wind banged against the car in a wave of dust and dirt. Maggie righted the car again, frightened by the power of the wind. She couldn't see anything but dust whipping across in front of her. She slowed to a crawl. The mountains to the east were a dark presence but it would be a long time before they would be able to see the snow-capped peaks in the sky. Maggie had not seen another car going by for the past twenty miles, so she drove faster and made good time. She was singing along to a Fats Domino tune about a blueberry hill when she reacted to something and threw on the brakes.

"What's the matter?" asked Eddie sleepily.

"Are you awake? I think something happened over there."

"Where?" He sat up and tried to see through the windshield.

"I don't know. I saw a flash of light." She drove more slowly, trying to see ahead through the darkness and the wind. Finally they saw what must have been the lights of the Trocadero. And nearby there were flashing lights on the highway. They could hear thunder above the noise of the engine.

"I think there's been an accident."

"Where? I don't see anything," said Eddie. They got closer to the flashing red lights.

"I think it's a bus." She could see the rear of a travel bus, red and yellow taillights flashing. And the black shape of a car sticking out from in front. The vehicles were on the access road to the Trocadero. Maggie swung the Buick over and drove along the shoulder. She had the indecipherable impression of a large black American car. Almost at the same time in the headlights of the Buick she saw that the door on the driver's side of the Ford had been torn off and astounding in its clarity was a human leg in driving position, motionless. But Eddie was screaming, "It's the Ford! It's the Ford!" It was hard to stop the car because people were milling all over. Finally she parked and pulled Eddie out with her from the driver's side and he stumbled towards the Ford and stopped, confused, because there was no way to get to Fernando and Bale: the front of the car was a twisted mess of compressed metal piled into the front seat. The top of the car where their heads had to be was a jumble of canvas and sharp edges of torn steel. Only Bale's leg clad in Levi's was too visible. The foot, the sock hanging down, the skin torn from the foot was too visible. She wanted to rush forward and cover it up; it was as if he were naked before strangers and didn't know it.

Eddie was crying like a small boy, crying and choking off his sobs. The bus driver was leaning towards them in the dust and smoke, holding up his hands in a questioning way and repeating, "They're dead. They're dead." Maggie looked up and saw an old Mexican woman looking down at them from the window of the bus. She was holding a handkerchief to her mouth. It was then that Maggie thought that she should act in some way equal to what was happening. But she moved like someone she didn't know, pointing her eyes in the direction she wanted to go and walking. She was holding on to Eddie so tightly her fingers were aching. She wanted them to hurt. She wanted to grip the cloth so hard she would be able to identify the texture down to the very threads.

A short moustachioed Highway Patrolman with narrow blue eyes came and talked to them. There was nothing to do but wait for a special crew to come and cut away the bus and the bodies from the car, and in the meantime he wanted to know if they had been drinking. Maggie was not sure if he meant her and Eddie or the men in the Ford and she tried to say a lot at once; her mouth wouldn't work right: "A beer, yes...two times, two copas, and coffee and tortillas...maybe one beer and one copa...but that was a long time ago, that's how the tortillas..."

"How old are you? How much did you drink? How much did they drink?"

"We were celebrating because of the Brahmas, earlier." Eddie stopped. His eyes were almost closed against the dust.

"Do you know you're not legal drinking age?" They were trying to speak to each other in the middle of a wind storm.

"We were across the border," Maggie shouted.

"I don't care where you were. All of you think you can do anything you want over there and then come over here and scatter your wrecks all over U.S. highways." The wind was tearing the words from his mouth and throwing them in her face.

"Mexicans aren't the only ones dying on this highway," Maggie shouted back.

His face was in her face. "You're in the United States of America now and you've been drinking illegally and I didn't say anything before because you said it was his brother but your attitude stinks, girl."

Maggie was shaking inside from anger as well as pain. "You stink and your job stinks too!" she shouted. She knew she had pushed him hard because he spit, "You get in the car" at Eddie, pushing him towards the patrol car, and at her, coldly and evenly, "I can take both of you in for drunk driving. I can have your car impounded and I'll do it if you open your mouth one more time. Do I make myself clear?"

She wouldn't say yes, and instead spun away and left him standing there holding his clipboard, his fancy fur collar up around his ears.

She wanted to wail for Bale and at the same time could not display her grief before anyone. Her tears were a hard rock inside her breast and it was hard to keep from choking as she walked to the arriving ambulance. She told them not to take the bodies back to the border—they were from El Pueblo. She told them what mortuary. She found out what the families would have to do later. She wrote down what decisions had to be made, what information had to be given. She did the things no one else was there to do. Then she went to Eddie in the cop car. He was huddled in the back seat, knees up against his chin. The wind rocked the car, trying to turn it over. "Wait until he says you can get out," she told him.

"He's gonna keep me here."

"Naw, he won't." But she wasn't completely sure. She fought her way back to the Buick, running the heater, trying to get warm. The wind storm was on top of them now but nothing else happened; there was only wind. She was thinking they should be together, her and Eddie. She was just getting out of the car to go to him when the Highway Patrolman walked up and motioned to her. She ran over and waved to Eddie through the window. The cop talked to them about notification. But she told him, "His mother's alone. There's no phone. Don't send anyone. He'd better tell her, and his cousin's family." Eddie was not able to talk. His eyes were slits from exhaustion and crying.

As they started to drive out, the cop hit the side of the car door with his hand. They were startled, frightened. But he only wanted to tell them to drive carefully.

Maggie drove, but her mind kept going backwards to when Bale wasn't dead. She wanted time to go back, but it kept going forward and the longer Bale was dead, the deader he got; the more real the fact of his death became. And now they were sick with knowing it. Maggie drove with an arm around Eddie, trying not to stare at the road, but she was afraid to blink. She felt like a child, afraid to close her eyes even for a second or death might grab her too. In the hour before dawn the wind subsided. The last few stars shone pristine in the sky as they reached El Pueblo. The empty streets looked like they had when she was little. She wanted it to be when they were growing up, the three of them chasing each other around the watermelon vines at La Milpa. She drove over the bridge and it could have been for the first time—the familiar had become strange with death. Thin wisps of smoke from nighttime fires rose from among the shacks along the river. The sky was now an unbelievable pink, low-lying clouds blue against the mountains. A small bird darted over their heads as they got out of the car.

"Do you want me to wait?"

"No."

"You're going to need a car."

"Fernando's father has one." He took a deep breath. "It's hard to...tell her." His face twisted with grief. Maggie put her arms around him, held him.

"Do you want me to come in with you?"

"No, I better do it alone."

"I'll be home all day."·

"Naw...don't. It's okay." Tears were standing again in his eyes. She waited until he had walked away, then went and stood on the bridge. The sky was changing with each passing moment. She looked over at La Milpa. She saw the corrugated metal walls, the bits and pieces of unmatched plywood, the crooked smokestacks leaning from the wind. She had not really looked at it for a long time or maybe she had never looked at it like this, from the outside. And now she couldn't stand to see how poor it was because it reminded her of everything he never had, of Bale. She couldn't stand to see how it was. She looked instead at the riverbed. She studied the beautiful designs made in the earth by the rain and flowing water. There were still a few deep spots where the water was standing, dark and silent. It was so quiet everywhere. It was true what Grandmother said, she thought. This place was finished. La Milpa would be erased, its last harvest of laughter and grief given back to the skies. She turned away from the river, heard her bootheels tapping on the wooden bridge. She walked to the car and got in stiffly. Every feeling she had, every move she made was final. Los Quates was big and brown and rough in the morning light. It looked bigger than it had seemed to her as a child, but that couldn't be.

As Maggie was driving past the Mission she saw women in rebozos and children with slicked-down hair climbing the wide steps for six o'clock Mass. She was startled by the sonorous ringing of church bells giving the five minute warning. Each fact, each thing that occurred struck her deeply with its distinctness, its individuality, its unrelatedness. She pulled over to the curb. The Mission doors were open and she could see all the way to the altar, splendid in gold and candlelight. She could not see the faces of the saints and she was glad. She could not ask for anything or excuse anything. "People have good instincts," Bale had said, "they go to church, but they only really want to go at Christmas and Easter." Life and death, death and life over and over and over again, take a breath, let it out. He had always blurred the edges, making everything big and then telling her to look at it. And she had always looked at specific little things, hanging on to the particular while things crashed down around her. But this time, this time she was alone. Thoughts came and went...nothing to think about. Then what was choking her so badly? She gripped the steering wheel and stepped on the gas and made the car go around the corner away from the Mission and away from El Pueblo. At that instant the sun cleared the face of La Madre, evaporating the dew on thorns of saguaro and ocotillo all over the desert in one long gathering flashing second of light.

Chapter 27

▲

Maggie drove into the desert over a new road, not yet paved but carved wide and smooth out of the red earth. There were new homes here and there atop a hill. But she found an isolated place, a ravine flanked by curving lomitas. She backed the car into a small wash out of sight of the road. She walked east following the natural course of the ravine. Above her there was thick underbrush and over that the sky was a fierce blue. She couldn't go far but dropped heavily to the sand in a spot the sun had not touched yet. The ground was moist and as cold as the air which was scented by roots and decaying grasses. She leaned back and after some time stretched out her legs, digging her bootheels into the ground. The birds were chirping but it hurt to hear them. Nothing was forever. She had seen the dead flesh, the congealed blood; she had received a wound to the heart. She curled up against the sand trying to feel only what was beneath her. The sun broke the shadow she was in but she was not aware of it. Clouds had come over the mountains and rose bright and white and full, playthings in the sky. Later on, they became thin nebulous grey shapes and the wind lay them down against the hills. The sun went in and out and Maggie jerked awake sweating and cold just in time to see the rain begin to fall. It was racing across the hills and she opened her face to it, willing it to get closer but the rain resisted. She stood against the biting wind but she felt only her heart thudding beneath her breast. Once she could fly into the stars but now she was carved immobile. Her tears were falling far away and even flapping sparrows did not wait. They were gone to meet the rain that was dancing, dancing on the crest of the hill.

Chapter 28

▲

Doreen came up to Maggie at school. "My mother says I can go to the wake."

"Great."

"Is there anything I should do?"

"You have to cover your head. Wear a scarf."

"Can we go together?" For once Doreen seemed small and insecure.

"Sure."

The bare undecorated room was full. The families were in their best clothes. Eddie wore a jacket she had never seen before; Maggie wondered if it had belonged to Bale. His mother was wailing, "Mi hijo, mi hijo," swaying dangerously on the folding chair. Eddie hovered beside her and the face he turned to them was tear-stained, but he was not crying. Maggie and Doreen moved past them, following the others to the front of the room. Maggie was not aware if there were any flowers. Relatives from across the border were standing and milling around Fernando's family but somehow the people arranged themselves to pass the two coffins one by one. She knew instinctively which one was Bale, although the figure lying there did not resemble him; only the slant of the eyes was familiar. His hair had been combed back from his forehead and he wore a white shirt buttoned to the throat. The black coat, sleeves too long for his arms, was not like him either. Maggie glanced at Fernando; his reddish hair was also strange on the yellow satin of the pillow beneath his head.

Afterwards, Maggie took Doreen to the bus station to catch her bus to the east side. She did not want to wait with her but drove directly to the shooting range. She wanted to be alone and separate from even herself. She put on the earphones and walked downstairs into the long narrow metal box of the shooting range. Most of the alleys were empty—too early in the day—so she took the one on the far side where no one would come. She slapped a few shells into the chamber of the rifle without counting them. From standing position she fired one after the other without putting up a target, just pumping the trigger and feeling the pressure of the stock against her shoulder, hearing the muffled pops of the explosions. Then she pinned up a target, walked back and loaded some more shells. She practiced standing and kneeling, much more difficult positions than lying down. She concentrated on breathing and squeezing the trigger. She fired at the target until the center was torn out of it, then threw it aside and put up another. She already had a full rack of sharp-shooter bars. They hung on a nail above her bed. She fired at will, changing positions often and at random. She fired and loaded and fired until the barrel was an extension of her arms and eyes and the trigger worked in unison with her brain. At the end her body was shaking all over as if from the cold and she stopped. She packed up the remaining shells and cleaned up the range of targets and wasted cartridges.

It was dark when she came out onto the street, barely able to stand. Her shoulder was sore and beaten and she was stiff all over, and shaking with fatigue that made it hard to even walk. She went to bed without eating. She rolled herself in a wool blanket and at last fell asleep.

En La Tarde

Bueno, hija, aquí nos encontramos de nuevo.
En esta soledad no viven mentiras. Yo sabía
que me ibas a pedir unas respuestas pero ya
encontraste la verdad no? Que las palabras
para bien o para mal pueden definirlo a uno.
Que los cuentos se paran y andan.

Y entonces?

In The Afternoon

So my daughter, we meet again. In this solitude lies cannot live. I knew that you would
expect some answers from me but you have
already found the truth, right? That words,
for good or for evil, can make us what we are.
That stories stand up and walk.

    And now?

Chapter 29

▲

This day was chosen. Today the birds were singing because they were happy in the warm weather. The sun shone brightly in a clear sky, sending the morning dew running. There would be many more days after this with fresh and lucid skies.

Adela Sewa took a velís from under her bed. It was a very old one made of tin and tied with a strong rope. She carefully took out the things she had been saving, each one wrapped in tissue paper. She put underwear, petticoat and silk stockings side by side upon the bed. Then she took down her bandeja and carried it outside for this important bath.

In a sheltered place where the orange trees grew and the golden rays of the sun came, she bathed herself with cold water. She examined every aspect of her flesh, the scars and broken places of a lifetime. She cleaned her body carefully and respectfully, each act completed before proceeding to the next. She rinsed her hair with juice squeezed from a lemon. The peelings she lay on top of the adobe wall to dry in the sun and scent the air. The tub was rinsed, the bar of white soap rewrapped in its paper.

After the underwear was on, Adela Sewa sat on the edge of the bed, as she had always done, to put on silk stockings, knotting each one just above the knee. Then, arranging the hairpins beside her, she combed her hair slowly and made two long braids, deciding at the last minute to leave them hanging down. Her fingers did the thing they had practiced many times, taking a ribbon that had lain on the altar and tying her braids with it to lie on her back. "Qué fuerte eres," she murmured to the frag-ment of red ribbon. Her hands lingered over the stitches of the new pintito made for this occasion. The long sleeves were gathered at the cuff, the buttons made by hand from ironwood. The long simple skirt was black and reached to her ankles. At last she tied a necklace made of turquoise beads and onyx around her neck. Then she went outside to collect a few rose petals from each of her bushes, which she put in her pocket.

She had done everything according to her way and to her liking. She sat down in front of her altar, gazing in silence at the burnt earth which had become what it was from so many years of meditations and prayers. She had truly loved this piece of earth made from the body of La Madre when she was still strong enough to carry the earth home in sacks from the mountain. Mixing the dirt with alfalfa stubble from the fields, she had made adobes, one by one, with her hands and feet, herself baking in the sun along with the brick. Many times flame and wax had scorched the altar, the earth hardening, the adobe polish-ing. She passed her hands over the surface for the last time, leaving her feelings in the stone. Her memories were like wild birds set free and rising to the wingbeat of her blood, each one returning to rest in its place on the trail of her life. So she walked slowly around her house, blessing and thanking each thing that had served her in life. Her pots and few dishes she took leave of as from old friends. Each one she praised and petted and put in the box by the door to be taken away by the peddler who passed by each month. Smoothing the door that opened to her touch, she said goodbye and locked it, leaving the key beneath a rock. Her jars of yerbas and bellota she had already given away. She was free. And Maggie would not have to say goodbye a hundred times: everything that had her personal touch upon it had been taken care of. Maggie was still in her thoughts, daughter of her heart. The drops of milk that gave Maggie life had not come from her breast.

Adela Sewa arranged her tapalo about her head so that it fell just above her eyes. She had chosen the deep red rebozo, not the black one. "For I am not going to a funeral," she thought and smiled. There was nothing to hold her now. Her real name did not exist anywhere in the world; nothing would appear in the newspaper about her. The trees—the lemon, the orange, the pomegranate—these knew her name because they had spoken with her, but they would not tell anybody. The beauty of a flickering candle flame and the beauty of silence held her attention. These too she would let go, together with the child she had loved from the first day to this last day. She had filled her hands with gifts and Maggie must learn to take or to ignore them—that was her life to make and to choose. Now Adela Sewa had no more attachment there. She had done everything in her style, according to her liking, ever since she had opened to Death on the window mountain. Since then she had freed herself step by step until now.

El Cuento:

Y ahora iba cerrando la mujer la puerta del cerco cuando notó que venía una y que venía arrastrando un pie. Sin querer, ésta tuvo que ponerse contra el cerco.

Acercándose, la mujer le levantó la cabeza y vió que venía un venado herido en cuerpo humano. Entonces a ésta que se estaba desmayando, le dió las rosas que traía en la bolsa. Y para su pie herido, se quitó sus medias de seda y se las amarró en el pie. Así fue que el venado tuvo la fuerza de brincar de un golpe y de llegar al monte.

The Story:

And now the woman was closing the door to the fence when she noticed that someone was coming and that this person was dragging a foot. Without choosing to, the person had to lean against the fence. Getting near her, the woman lifted the head and saw that there was a wounded deer in this human body. Then, to the one who was fainting, she gave some roses that were in her pocket. And for the wounded foot, she took off her silk stockings and tied them around it. In this way it happened that the deer had the strength to spring all at once and to reach the mountains.

When Adela Sewa sees the deer going, she understands that this is the trail she must follow to the heart of the mountain. Then she hears someone say, "Still saving babies and animals, I see." La Muerte is leaning against the fence where the deer has been, grinning. Then Death jumps over the fence with an indescribable show of flashing garments. Adela Sewa watches this ostentatious action with compassion also.

"You aren't needed this time," she says.

"I know, but I wanted to come anyway. To see what you did last." Thus saying, La Muerte becomes a skeleton.

"Ahhhhh," says Adela Sewa. At that moment she sees the Buick approaching. Its white and chrome exterior shines like a polished mirror and a crepe paper banner in celebration of this day is flying from the antenna. Grandmother turns to La Muerte.

"Don't worry, I'll ride in back," the skeleton says.

Maggie lowers the top. The turquoise seats gleam softly as Grandmother gets in. La Muerte has the whole back seat.

And so, Maggie, her yellow hair standing up on her head like the headdress of a princess, Adela Sewa, wearing her favorite red rebozo, and La Muerte, who lays claim to the crepe paper banner, waving it beautifully in the wind, ride gaily and solemnly towards the east where La Madre waits with open arms.

Chapter 30

▲

"Margarita Conners"—it was there in the program in black and white. Her mother was in the audience with her nina. Mariana was smiling, her wavy hair combed smoothly back from her forehead. Maggie had dressed and combed and powdered her mother's face before getting ready herself. Mariana looked almost like she had years ago, before she got sick. Emma was beside her, older and more frail, with a handkerchief in her hand which she used to pat her neck now and then. It was warm under the bright football field lights.

Maggie looked away from them over the sea of graduating seniors in caps and gowns. She looked around for Eddie just in case he had come, but she didn't see him. She was aware of the other ninety-nine seniors on the platform with her, proud and nervous to be in the top one hundred of the graduating class. They were perhaps a little more serious than the rest, carrying a responsibility which they didn't all want for being smart. They were mostly male faces and a number of Chinese faces. There was no one who looked like Maggie. In the long months since Bale's death and Grandmother's leaving, her eyes had set deeply into her face, accentuating the slant and darkness of those eyes. Her face was thin and, in spite of the hat Mariana always gave her to wear, dark from the sun. Her short hair too was bleached almost white from the sun. Her chest and shoulders were beginning to fill out, to be in proportion with the long stride of her legs. The years of chopping wood and scrubbing clothes on a washboard had built strength into her arms. But she was pretty only when she smiled; at other times her mouth was too tight, her face too inflexible and serious and her feelings too hidden behind her eyes. She sat without listening to the words of the speakers, thinking her own thoughts. She reached for a stub of pencil in her pocket and scratched out the name "Conners." She wrote in the margin, "Margarita Forté." It was her mother's name. It would now be hers. She was able to sit quietly through the rest of the ceremony and then it was over, the boys throwing their hats high in the air. They sailed, red tassels catching the light, unexpectedly beautiful as they came down.

She got through the crowds of congratulating parents and friends to where Mariana stood with Emma. They both embraced her. Her nina handed her a small package. Inside the brown paper bag was a gift wrapped in tissue paper with a pink ribbon around it. The tissue paper and ribbon had seen other wrappings, Maggie knew: the sisters threw nothing away. She opened it. Inside were two pairs of nylon stockings. *"Para cuando vas a Misa.* For when you go to Mass," Nina said. Maggie pressed a kiss to the wrinkled cheek her nina offered and thanked her again.

Graduation night! She saw Doreen from a distance with a good-looking guy in Airman's uniform, but she made no attempt to get their attention. Well, it was really over at last. Everybody would be out celebrating, dancing. If Bale were here…She turned to Emma who was telling her what they had prepared at the house in her honor.

Maggie wore the cap and gown into the house so Josepha could see how she looked. As Maggie climbed the ancient steps and went inside, a memory from her child-hood came vividly to mind. It was of the three sisters getting ready to go to church. They all wore their hair in the same style: parted in the middle and held in a bun in the back with hairpins. Just before going out the door, they wet their fingers and patted their hair in front into waves. Then when all were ready, they made a dash for the Mission, usually arriving in time for the five minute bell. But sometimes it sounded when they were still on the way, and then they ran! The three could be seen hurrying along in single file. The swiftest of the three was Josepha and the most determined to get there on time. Behind her came Emma. She always had her wits about her, properly attired in tapalo and rebozo, but simply wasn't very fast. And last of all, behind her ran Consuelo, large and heavy with her hair and clothes in disarray, trying to wrap her rebozo around her as she went. They all met at the door of the Mission in order to go in together.

Maggie looked through the window, trying to see the comal under the ramada. It was no longer used, but it reminded her of Consuelo and she wished with all her heart that she was here. Still, she was glad to see the other faces she had known throughout her life gathered around. Josepha had opened the door to the sala because this was a special evening and she went to her room to get the bottle of brandy she kept hidden in the closet. She poured some into each cup of chocolate and everyone toasted Maggie and wished her well. She was now a woman in their eyes, a woman who would care for her mother, a woman who would go to work in the world. They did not know about Maggie's plans to go to college. Later on, when they were alone, she would explain to her nina.

That night, when she was at home with Mariana, she came to her mother's room and saw her sitting quite still by the window. She was suddenly taken with fear, the fear she had never allowed expression during those years when Mariana did not speak or seem to see her. She knelt by her mother's chair. "Don't go, just don't go," she whispered.

"I was asleep," Mariana said, "and I dreamed that I was painting the windows and I was asking you, what color?"

"Any color you want," said Maggie. "It's up to you." Mariana laughed with her, and, reassured, she got ready for bed without protest. Maggie was already in her boots and Levi's to go out.

"Where?"

"Don't worry, Mama, I'm just going for a ride. Maybe I'll see some of the kids but I'll probably just ride around."

"Good, but don't come home too late." Maggie stayed with her until she was asleep. At the last minute she took the tassel with her, putting it into the pocket of her jacket. She left the lamp burning low like her mother liked and went out, locking the gate after her.

She stood for a moment by the car enjoying the moon. It was big and yellow in the sky. Then she started the Buick and drove slowly down the dirt road to the new highway that went around El Pueblo. She headed north-east, following the moon. Soon she had passed the main part of town. Only a solitary light flashed sometimes on the lower slopes of the mountains. She turned north, climbing, and headed for the back side of the Santa Teresas. She had been to this place only once, the year before, with Balestine. They had gotten stuck in a tight switchback. Part of the road had fallen off on the cliff side and a stout tree was still gripping the mountain road with its roots. They had finally maneuvered Bale's Ford around and got it pointed downhill again after some hair-raising stops and starts. She found the place without difficulty and stopped near some mounds of dirt that marked the road's end. She leaned back to watch the moon and listen to the night around her. She remembered the tassel and pulled it out of her pocket, smoothing the threads with her fingers. She hung it on the rearview mirror, then got out and started walking down the road. She climbed over the mountain of dirt and scuttled down the other side, looking for the clearing she had been in before. It was a place of lush grassland, beautiful and untouched, in the middle of just rock. The night was sweet and warm enough to be able to walk comfortably. Her boots crunched as she walked on the quartz and sandstone to the grassy meadow. The mountain was alive with insect sound. Mountain lions would not come down this far so early in the summer. There was still plenty of water and game in the high places and it was too cold for rattlers to be hunting at night. But she watched the ground ahead anyway as she walked, swinging her eyes in a full circle back and forth. A large mound of sandstone stood out against the mountain. The rounded shapes on top suggesting form piled on form, carved for countless years by the powerful desert winds. Maggie climbed up on a boulder and looked around for any sign of movement. She saw and heard nothing unrecognizable. Then she dropped down on the meadow.

She did not really see it at first because it was the last thing she expected to find and because the moonlight was momentarily obscured by fleeting cloud. But when she came to the edge of the grass she also came up against a high wooden fence separating her from the meadow.

Maggie walked straight up to the fence, looking at it incredulously. She looked along its length and saw it stretching far into the darkness on both sides. "A little fence, more or less," she said. She might have just climbed over it but she didn't. She ran at the fence and slammed into it with the full weight of her boots. She kicked and wrenched until her leather gloves were mangled. She kicked at the bottom rail until a piece came apart under her foot and she used it to swing at the rest. When she began to weaken and the fence was still standing, she ran towards it with her shoulder and crashed through to the other side. There she fell painfully to the ground. She lay with her arms flung out on the ground, face down in the soft wet grass of the meadow, and cried. She cried for Bale and for Grandmother, and most of all for the vanishing freedom and spiritual life of the desert. She cried until she could stand to breathe without them. And then she sat up slowly and wiped her face on the tails of her shirt.

Nothing was different. The stars were the same, pouring their radiance down on the meadow. The mountain rose in splintered spires of rock towards the sky. The pinion trees whispered harmoniously among themselves. The crickets sang a scratchy song.

Maggie got up and limped across the meadow to the drop-off on the other side and looked over the edge. On the far curve of the horizon, another mountain range melted into the sky. Down on the plain, smelter fires burned night and day, melting copper. She gave as much love as she could to the earth and took as much love as she could. Then she went back to the fence. She picked up the pieces of railing and put them back together. She pounded the nails in with a rock. She went to the car and got some wire to tie the broken pieces together. She looked over her efforts to restore the fence with a wry smile. She knew she would not come back to see what became of this meadow. But she wouldn't forget how the plains were shaped, or how the curve of the earth looked under a full moon. Everything would continue to live in the fertile ground of her feelings.

Chapter 31

▲

It was early morning three years later. Maggie drove the Buick to the foothills of Las Tinajas far to the south. She went off the road into the desert for several miles and stopped near a small rise and got out of the car. The sky was just beginning to turn purple. The last stars sparkled like brittle glass and went out. Maggie was hollow and stretched too tight from too little sleep, too much energy expended. She knew that if she stuck it out the feeling would go away. But it was cold. She was shivering in a thick sweater and Levi jacket. Even in leather gloves her hands were freezing. She shoved them deep into her pockets and waited out the last of the darkness.

She heard the cry of an owl flying home to roost. She saw it glide to the tallest saguaro. And with this, dawn came: purple lightened to pink and then to true grey. With shoulders hunched she waited for the sun to rise, moving her feet against the cold. She had planned to be well on the trail by now, but it no longer seemed important to hurry or keep to any previous plan. The sun's rays close to the ground felt warmer than they would later and she needed to feel warm right now. She drank only a small amount of water and fastened the canteen back on her belt. The sun was fully up and she was ready.

As soon as she swung onto the trail and into a climbing rhythm, she felt stronger. After half an hour she came up on the horse corrals and a few minutes later crossed the creek, thick with grass. This part of the trail was gentle. She stopped at the beginning of steep ground to look down the way she had come. The corrals were below her. Very soon the vaqueros would be shouting and whistling, swinging their lariats, and the mustangs and quarter horses would be milling and raising the dust. But this early it was quiet, patches of mist clinging to the shadows. The vaqueros were just bringing out the saddles; the horses were reluctant to move.

The ascending trail was narrow and steep and continually switching directions. Skinny pinion trees and saplings grew along the edges by twisting their roots deep into the rocks. Maggie put head and shoulders into the climb and soon, her feet reading it first, came to the slight depression that marked the end of the first leg of the trail. She dropped her pack and lay down flat on the ground. She put her legs up against a boulder and breathed as deeply as she could. After a few moments, her breath came more slowly and her heart was not beating so fast. She rested, putting her arms behind her head and looking up at the colorless sky. Then she stood up and leaned out against a scrub oak to see the desert far below.

Low-lying clouds lay like sleeping snakes along the horizon. The bowl-like curve of the earth and mountains faded away to the west. At this height, the identity of the immediate desert was already in question. She recognized the rising face of La Madre to the north, but the desert beneath her was transformed into an array of shapes and textures. It appeared purely geometrical. She was suddenly seized by dizziness and holding on to the young sapling with both hands, she carefully moved one foot at a time away from the edge. With shaking hands she unfastened straps, took out food and ate. She concentrated on chewing and swallowing. It was stupid to let herself get like this, but she had not been able to sleep. She let herself drift, motionless.

The passing of time, the responsibilities of getting an education and surviving financially, of taking care of the ranchería and Mariana, the forming of a new, important friendship—all this had not taken away what she felt at each anniversary of Grandmother's leaving. She was scrambling all the time to finish it. Sometimes she was not even sure that everything had happened the way she remembered. Something always pursued her, gave her unrest. An indefinite thing or place that could never quite get real but would not go away. A diagram: black marks in a white space that nevertheless had form and one edge pointing directionally. Yes, she knew there was the ring; every time she looked at it she was reminded of that day when Grandmother had called her to her side. She had brought out a pañuelo tied in knots. Inside there were some things: an ancient medicine bottle with part of a string of pearls; a tiny woven basket with a few gold coins; a beautiful ring of white gold with four small diamonds and a transparent blue stone. But it was this other ring that Maggie had chosen, the one with the picture on it. It was a ring of silver and turquoise and two bands of coral like veins of blood. It was a picture of a mountain with wings flying out on both sides. And the ring had brought her here.

She saw Grandmother again the way she had stood on the trail of La Madre. Her face had changed. There were no longer personal feelings reflected in it. But she had said, "I am going. There's no more. I have given you all I could. Now you must make your life...." Her words became indistinct. And Maggie had answered, "I want to stay with you." Grandmother said something but Maggie could not understand it, and then she could not speak. She could not find the right words to make Grandmother stay. Step by step, Grandmother had climbed higher and farther away. Maggie waited for her to turn around...hips moving in slow motion...Grandmother reached the top of the switchback and without a wasted gesture was gone.

Maggie knew that she had been a child then. Now she was traveling in order to understand more. Now she was leading herself, and she went on following the trail and eventually reached Los Pinos, a place where a cluster of pines stood and water ran in a shallow stream. A slight breeze stirred the treetops and two squirrels chased each other and disappeared in the thick branches. Maggie decided not to stay long. It was almost midday and larger animals might be coming to drink. So she refilled her canteen and returned to the trail on the ridge that ran up and over this oasis along the cliff. Several long hours later she came out on a mesa near the top of the northern wing of the mountain. The air here was thicker with low cloud cover. It was colder and it would soon rain. She found the overhang where others had sheltered before. There were black rocks arranged in a rough circle at the entrance. A bright spot in the clouds above showed the position of the sun. She took out a rain poncho and, after taking another look at the sky and testing the direction of the wind, put it on. She could not hear any thunder.

She spent some time gathering fuel, pine branches brought down by rain and high winds. She dragged them to the shelter and quickly broke a few with her hatchet. She pulled apart some shreds of bark and started a fire. It was already raining and she sat with her back to the rock and watched the rain. It was only a fine drizzle and would probably stay that way. She warmed herself and kept watch. The rain fell straight down. There was no wind to make it wave and it was easy to see all the way to the rocks at the edge of the mesa. She fell asleep and slept deeply for a long time. When she awakened, the fire was smoldering coals. She brought it back up just to see the flame. She was warm enough still and the rain had stopped. She could not see any stars. But the moon was moving behind the clouds. It was not dark but it was impossible to tell the time of day or night. She took a few steps and then a few more onto the mesa and then she saw that she was standing on a trail she had never seen before but it was where she was supposed to be: Grandmother stood on the trail ahead of her. Grandmother spoke but her words were incomprehensible. Maggie lay down on the ground, arranging her body in the correct posture for speaking with the dead.

"This is the last time you will see me. After this your dreams will be only remembrances of me," the form that was Grandmother said. Her hair was white and fell back from her forehead. Her clothes shone brighter than the moon. Maggie looked at her feet and Grandmother said, "You see how beautiful the shoes you have brought me, my daughter." Then she gestured to Maggie to stand up and she saw a small tent pitched on the trail.

"You will not be alone," Grandmother said. "I will stay with you all night, but when dawn comes I will be far from here." Far distant, on top of the mountain, it was as if daylight. A hawk circled and fell and fell and gently came to rest where another hawk waited, and someone sat nearby and lifted the hawks, one on each wrist, and flung them back into the sky. Maggie was only a witness to this, to see that the mountain grew out of the picture on her ring. The hawks stretched turquoise wings and flew in an immense sky that seemed never to come to earth except at her feet.

"Do not be afraid. At the end, words return to nothing, as they are before they are spoken." The mountain held Grandmother with its wings but her feet touched the ground where Maggie stood. She saw this ground was a sacred place and many Beings were here together and shouted with the keening of hawks. Their voices rose and swept everything away. Tall buildings of brick and glass shimmered and faded like burning cellophane. English words, Spanish words were bodiless echoes. Silver conchos lighted plastic highways and adobe walls fell on crosses painted pink and blue and yellow. They fell to nothing without a sound, without raising a speck of dust. She could cease to mourn. She could stop running. She could understand. The red stone was her own life. She tasted the bitter flavor of sage. Rain came out of her mouth and fell on the earth of her body, but she had already heard the hoofbeats of a horse. The Great White Horse rose from the skeleton of the earth and carried her. She saw many people, many women walking together. They were going towards the stars. She saw the rain curving beautifully along the ridges and lomitas of the desert. She knew that Grandmother waited for her there along the low black peaks of home and Maggie cried out, but she turned the horse and rode on. The Great White Horse moved without effort on a trail that opened...opened...opened.

It was still the evening of the same day when Maggie opened her eyes and saw the mesa, serene, peaceful, spread out under the red rays of the setting sun. The sky had cleared in the west. A light snow had fallen, enough to hold hoofprints, and she followed them to the mesa's edge in time to see a burning orange ball of sun sink beneath the horizon. A few bands of cloud remained and were colored oven-red. The desert was swept with unbroken bands of pink fading far in the east to a subtle, heartrending emerald green.

She sat and pensively watched the night sky appear. The first stars came out. She went to the overhang and made a new fire, took some food and water and then, wrapped up in her poncho, lay down under the moving stars.

Al Oscurecer

Ya ves, hija, el camino que sigue también vuelve.

At Nightfall

You see, my daughter, the road going is also
the one coming back.

Glossary

▲

altiplano — high plateau
bailes — dances
bajada — descending slope
bandeja — a wide deep pan
barranca — ravine
bellota — acorn
cajitas — little boxes
calles — streets
carne asada — roasted meat
cascabel — rattle snake
centavos — pennies
chavalas — kids (girls)
chicharrón — fried beef tripe
cholla — a specific type of cactus
cholo — peasant
chucata — mesquite sap (colloquial)
Cien Milla — Hundred Mile
comal — fireplace

conchos — small round beaten silver disks used for decoration on clothes

conejo con chile — rabbit with chili

copa — an alcoholic drink

corrido — ballad

cucarachas — cockroaches

curandera — healer

desayuno — breakfast

descanso — rest

Dios mío — my God

El Camino de Los Dioses — The Highway of the Gods

El Shonte — Mockingbird

las estaciones — small, unpopulated stops on a bus route

en la siesta — afternoon nap

esqueleto — skeleton

gringos — whites

guitarrón — a base guitar

hediondilla — wilderness (colloquial)

horita — right now

huaraches — sandals

huesero — bone man (healer)

"Indios cochinos" — "filthy Indians"

jacal — shack

la migra — immigration

La Milpa — The Place of Harvest (colloquial)

lámpara — lamp

lechuga — lettuce

leña — firewood

lomitas — hills

"Los años..." — "the years..."

'mano (hermano) — brother

masa — dough

menudo — a kind of soup

mesquite — a desert tree

mierda — shit

mi hijo — my son

muchachitos — little boys

mucho más — much more

muleta — a bull fighting cape

nada — nothing

nina — godmother

ocotillo — a specific type of cactus

Padrecitos — little priests

Padre — priest

padres — parents

palo verde — a desert tree

pan de huevo — egg bread

panocha — burned sugar

pañuelo — handkerchief

"para qué" — "what for"

pasillo — corridor joining houses

"pero la verdad es" — "but the truth is"

pintitos — grey and white design

pomadas — herbal salves

"porqué, linda?" — "why, pretty one?"

pozol — a type of stew (made of beans, hominy grits and beef)

primo tequila — the best tequila

puta — whore

"Qué fuerte eres" — "how powerful you are"

quedita — blondie

quelites — wild greens (colloquial)

quelites con frijoles guisados — wild greens with fried beans

ramada — a shady space created by the branches of trees or bushes

ranchería — ranch

rancherías chiquitas — small ranches

Ranchería de Las Hermanas — the sisters' ranch

rebozo — shawl

remolino — whirlwind

río — river

sala — living room

sarape — a large shawl

"Se hizo chicharrón" — "he made himself a chicharrón; he fried himself"

saguaro — a specific type of cactus

sauco — a specific type of tree

sillones — armchairs

sonsa — stupid

tapalo — scarf

"Tengo hambre" — "I'm hungry"

tiempo — time

turistas — tourists

vaqueros — cowboys

veladoras — candles placed in glass cups, specifically for use during prayers

velís — suitcase

viejitos — old ones

yerbas — herbs

Edna Escamill

▲

was born in Calexico, California, and grew up in southwestern Arizona and in Baja California, Mexico. "I have traveled past the crossroads y mis zapatos todavía tienen mucha suela! (and my shoes still have a lot of leather!)"

Photo by Eden

aunt lute books is a multicultural women's press that has been committed to publishing high quality, culturally diverse literature since 1982. In 1990, the Aunt Lute Foundation was formed as a non-profit corporation to publish and distribute books that reflect the complex truths of women's lives and the possibilities for personal and social change. We seek work that explores the specificities of the very different histories from which we come, and that examines the intersections between the borders we all inhabit.

Please write or phone for a free catalogue of our other books or if you wish to be on our mailing list for future titles. You may buy books directly from us by phoning in a credit card order or mailing a check with the catalogue order form.

Aunt Lute Books
P.O. Box 410687
San Francisco, CA 94141
(415) 826-1300